MA[illegible]

or

The Material

By the same author

Novels

NO ANSWER

THE INQUISITORY

BAGA *In preparation*

SOMEONE *In preparation*

Plays

Plays Volume 1: The Dead Letter, The Old Tune, Clope

Plays Volume 2: Architruc, Hypothesis, In Connection with Mortin *In preparation*

Robert Pinget

MAHU
or
The Material

A Novel

Translated by

Alan Sheridan-Smith

CALDER AND BOYARS
LONDON

First published in Great Britain 1966
by Calder and Boyars Ltd
18, Brewer Street, London, W.1.

First published in France 1952
by Les Editions de Minuit

Printed in Great Britain by
Unwin Brothers Limited
Woking and London

PART I

The Novelist

I

Warning

This is the story I can't make head nor tail of it, somebody said: "You ought to write it down," I can't remember who, perhaps it was me, I get everything mixed up, it's true sometimes when I'm being introduced to someone I concentrate so much I take on the same face as the person and the friend who is introducing us doesn't know if it's me or the other one, he just leaves me to sort it out for myself. Instead of saying: "Excuse me" and putting on my real face again I explain why I like to look like people and I get all mixed up again, my friend gets angry and the other person goes off saying she hasn't got all day to waste she's got shopping to do.

So I'm writing this story down but then there's Latirail, he writes novels. Sometimes he tells me how he does it, but I only get more confused, he explains about his characters but I might be one of them for all I know! It's all mixed up in my head, it doesn't do to think too much, you forget where you were, it's like fighting with the devil himself.

2

The Figs

I had to do something, you see. I was always being told to work. I used to hear them getting up at half-past six to go to the office. I had fourteen brothers. At twenty-five past six the one who had the alarm-clock woke up and went to wake the others. I'd hear him knocking very quickly at all their doors, so quickly it seemed as if he was knocking at the same door all the time. We lived in a hotel.

He'd miss my door. But I was always awake at quarter-past six. I used to wonder if one day he'd wake me like all the others and call: "The office!" My clothes were all laid out on the chair beside my bed. At twenty-past six I put my arm out of the bed and touched my trousers. Supposing he came and woke me too? I'd find myself in an office. I'd go to the boss and say: "They got me up at half-past six and here I am!" There're offices everywhere. Where we live you can't take two steps up the street without finding offices, people going to offices and offices looking for people.

Twenty-five past six. I can hear the alarm-clock. My brother will be getting up.

Half-past six. He's missed my door. I can put my hand back under the bedclothes. I can hear the others getting up, the taps being turned on, hot and cold water gas on every floor please do not wipe your razor-blades on the towels breakfast is served in the rooms the management is not responsible for the theft of articles that are not handed in at the reception desk. There used to be a tremendous noise on the landing at ten to seven. They were young then. They must have been about twenty. They liked to make a lot of noise. One of them nearly always shouted at my door: "Eh, Mahu, still asleep, lazybones?" Mother forbade them to open my door. She forbade them to wake me, she forbade them to talk to me about the office, she forbade them to make a noise. Gradually, as the years went by, the noise died down. I was no longer asked if I was asleep lazybones. I was allowed to put my arm out of the bedclothes and wait to see if they woke me. How many years ago was that, then? They must be thirty now.

Ten to seven. The taps are turned off. The windows are opened. The keys turn in the locks. Ever since we were twenty-five our doors have always been locked. The footsteps die away on the landing. The front door bangs. Not this time, then.

"Eh, Mahu! Are you asleep, lazybones?"

"What is it? Who's there?"

"It's me, Frédy."

"Who's Frédy?"

"The twelfth. Let me in."

I get up and open the door. Frédy's got a beard. He's wearing a handkerchief in his breast pocket. He's beginning to lose his hair. He looks like our father which art in heaven hallowed be thy name thy . . . I have to go and sit down on the bed. I'm trembling.

"What's the matter, Mahu?"

"Oh, nothing. I'm not used to it, that's all."

"Do you want a drink of water? Do you want some tea? Do you want an aspirin?"

"No, it's all right. Tell me about the office."

He sits down. He looks at his watch.

"That's just what I've come about. Don't tell Mother, but we need another clerk at the office. So I thought of you. You must get bored doing nothing all the time. What do you say?"

"Oh, yes! Thanks, Frédy! I'll get dressed right away."

"Hurry up, then. It's five to seven."

I who knew all the noises by heart, had listened to them so many times, taps being turned on hot and cold water, I couldn't do anything right. I opened the window, I cut the towel with my razor, I turned the gas on at every floor, I put my trousers on last. Frédy laughed. "You've got the behind of a baby," he said. "Hurry up, it's quarter-past seven." And we went out. But I remember, just before closing the door, just before, I couldn't help but look at my photograph. It was a photograph I'd taken of some figs one summer at Fontoine. A summer holiday. I felt . . . that's it, exactly like when you smoke your first cigarette of the day. I felt empty. I nearly collapsed. Frédy said: "What's the matter now?" And I said: "It's nothing. It's the figs."

I'm now a clerk at Juan Simon's. I don't go home any more. I sleep in the warehouse. I've found a place where the rain doesn't come in. I've got an old iron bed. I've stuck my photo of the figs on a plank opposite. At night a friend of mine comes here to sleep. He sleeps beside me on the floor covered in blankets and the tarpaulins of Simon's old car. So he doesn't get wet when it rains. He's a model at the Beaux Arts. He's a Hungarian or something of the kind. He says he loves me. When he says it too often I tell him he's getting on my nerves and he starts crying. I give him some honey that Mother brings sometimes. She's afraid I don't get enough to eat at Juan's, it's old honey she kept in reserve during the war for the customers at the hotel. It's gone all granulated. But I don't miss my room. All the others getting up in the morning, it was terrible . . . Now I get up at the same time as Traiko and we wash our hands and faces at the pump in the yard. He then goes off to have a cup of coffee—he goes to a different place every day. He gets it on credit. I get out my jar of honey. When I've finished I put it back under the bed. Then I go to the office.

Petite-Fiente is Juan Simon's daughter. She's eleven. She usually arrives at the office at the same time as me before going to school. She shows me the drawings she does and sums that are all wrong I think. I daren't correct them for her because I can't remember whether you put the figure you carry at the top or the bottom of the column. When I put it at the top the answer's not the same as when I put it at the bottom. Juan gives me parcels to take to the post office or to warehouses or to the station. I know how to use the weigh-bridge. I know how to fill up the labels with name of sender name of addressee weight nature of contents. I write it all down.

One day at about ten in the morning I happened to be outside Petite-Fiente's school. It was break-time. She saw me at the gates and called to me. She called her friends over and introduced me as "Mad Mahu". I wanted to smack her but I couldn't because of the gates. She's a nasty kid.

3

The Post Office

I was afraid I'd smacked Petite-Fiente.

You never know with her. She could quite easily say "He couldn't because of the gates" and pretend I hadn't smacked her. I went back to the school gates. Petite-Fiente was already well out of the way. I saw her friends. They started shouting "Here comes Mad Mahu who smacked Petite-Fiente." They put their tongues out at me and called me a dirty dog.

I didn't know what to do. Juan Simon was sure to give me the sack. No more warehouse, no more bed. I'd have to go home. I didn't want to. I had to find some way of staying at Juan's. I called at the post office to see if there were any letters to be collected. It was Sinture the Postmaster who invented the *poste restante*. You can't write directly to anyone. He forbade the postman to deliver letters. Everybody has to collect his own letters at the post office. Sinture gives them to you himself. He looks at you as you're reading them. You're not allowed to read them outside. If you do go outside to read them, he won't let you see your letters for at least two months.

There was one letter for me. It was from Petite-Fiente. It said: "Mahu, if you tell Papa you smacked me I'll tell him to sack you. Frédy says that if you're sacked you'll have to go back to the hotel. That would suit me. It would be a good thing if you did."

Things were looking better. At least I'd be able to stay at Juan's.

I had one more parcel to take to the station. I knew there was a letter inside. Juan sometimes tries to deal directly with customers he knows very well, so as not to have to go through Sinture. But it's dangerous. He's already been denounced by customers, or by employees opening parcels, or simply by secretaries replying "Thank you for your letter of the . . ." and the boss signs it without noticing. In the post office

Sinture sees Juan reading a letter which says "Thank you for your letter of . . .", so he knows that Juan must have sent a letter in the parcel that Sinture has not seen, so he won't let Juan see any of his letters for two months. It's very bad for Juan's business.

I knew my parcel contained a letter. I must be careful. But I was thirsty. I stopped at the Café du Cygne and ordered a *menthe à l'eau*. When I'm in a café, I daren't look at people, I'm afraid they'll suddenly say "You're not called Mahu" because when I was born I was given another name and I was always ill so they changed my name. Could that be called a lie? I think about it all the time.

When I had finished my *menthe à l'eau*, I saw that my parcel had disappeared. I looked everywhere, under the seats, under the chairs, the proprietor said he hadn't seen anything, I said it didn't matter unless it caused trouble for Juan at the post office. I went back to the office. Juan was lowering the iron shutters. "Good evening, Mahu. Oh, Mahu, I'm sorry about the bit of trouble you had with my daughter. Yes, yes, she told me she had smacked you. Please forgive her. She can be very nasty sometimes. Highly-strung, you know. It's all this worm-powder she's been taking!"

I think Sinture must have informed Juan by telephone and made him tell me that Petite-Fiente had told him.

4

Sinture

I'm very afraid when I go and see Sinture. He knows I hardly ever get any letters but I've got to talk to him. It's not very interesting what he tells me. He talks to me about different people who receive letters and I know quite a lot of them. He makes sure that what he says isn't interesting—almost as if he does it out of spite. He sits at his desk and says "Ah, my dear Mahu, and to what do I owe this pleasure?" and goes on sorting papers or doing accounts. I say I've come to see if there's any news but it's just to give him something to say. He says "Curious as ever! It's your great fault, my dear fellow. Where were we now?" And I say, for example, "The story of Petite-Fiente" or something else. He says "Oh, yes. I remember" and he tells me everything as if he was reading it, yes, he remembers everything. He never says "Would Petite-Fiente have done such-and-such a thing or would she have changed her mind?" he says "So what could I do? There were two solutions. I chose that one. This is why." And he tells me why and so on and so forth. How does he do it? What he says really isn't interesting. What is interesting is that he makes me afraid. He goes on with his typing or his accounts and says "Oh, yes, I'm behind everything, everything. I'm even writing your friend Latirail's novel. He writes down what I tell him. Take his story of the Lice Seekers, do you know what it is? It's simply the correspondence between young Pinson and Mlle Lorpailleur. The name Lorpailleur made him think of gold seekers and he changed it to lice seekers. And poor Pinson is dying of love for her."

He'll ruin Latirail's novel in the end, if only by whispering untruths in Mlle Lorpailleur's ear. She comes from a very good family, I've been told she writes novels at the university.

I wish I were Sinture for one thing: he knows everything at

once. He calls it unity. "The unity of a novel, my dear fellow," he says. "You don't think I could write a novel! I just lay the bait and let someone else do the writing. Don't tell Latirail about this." Of course I do tell Latirail about it because I find it very annoying that Sinture should tell him what to write. He says: "Tells me to write what? Do you think I'm a fool? Haven't you ever heard me arguing with that silly bugger Sinture?" It was no use trying to convince him that Sinture already knew the end of his novel, he said I must be out of my mind. It didn't bother him at all. But it frightens me. I think things like that are revelations.

I often think about Sinture with his pince-nez . . .

"You see that man over there?"

"Yes."

"It's my cousin. He died last year. I was very fond of him. He used to do a lot of reading, as Sinture would say. He read the *Imitation* a great deal. He was always saying "In the *Imitation* it says such and such a thing." It's a religious work. My cousin always went to Lourdes to do his *Imitation* I think. Can you see him? He hasn't recognised me yet. What's he got in his hand?

"The *Horizon-Mou.* The newspaper of Agapa."

"Ah, yes! I used to show that paper to Sinture when I came back from my holidays. He would say to me: 'You and your news of Agapa, it's nothing but idle gossip.' Which didn't stop him from reading it all the same and then mixing up all the news of Agapa with what happened here.'

Because he dictates novels to everybody, he also wants to dedicate them. He's already spoken about it to Latirail who said "Mind your own business, you old wind-bag".

But I wonder if he is right to snub him like that. Even if he doesn't think that Sinture dictates what he writes, supposing Sinture has his own revelations? Maybe he does. In any case he knows how the novels will end. And if he doesn't dictate them, who does write them exactly, exactly as he wishes? Latirail isn't bothered about it. I think it's dangerous. Sinture is a bore, of course, but even so, can we afford to just ignore him? He holds all the trumps, he invented the *poste restante*, he makes marriages, he's got novels. I daren't say he dictates them any more. But he dedicates them. He'll get his own way, in spite of Latirail. What is more, this is what he said to me about dedications: "When you dedicate books you tell people what you really think of them. In the case of Latirail's novel, for example, I shall say what I think of Mlle Lorpailleur. Not to mention young Pinson and the readers of Mlle Lorpailleur's novels and all the letters *poste restante* that gave birth to the Lice Seekers. There are a great many of these letters. It's not just a matter of the Pinson-Lorpailleur correspondence. Oh no. It's all the others as well, including those that Juan Simon puts inside parcels. When I say what I think of all these people I shall also be speaking for others. Do you imagine it's amusing dictating to fools? Now I shall get my own back a bit, you'll see. I don't mind telling you, in confidence, mind, that I loved Mlle Lorpailleur's mother. Her daughter might have taken after me. It was I who sent her to the University. I'm a bitter man, Mahu, a bitter man."

5

The Lice

I went and told Latirail that Sinture would dedicate his book whether he liked it or not. Ninette came to the door. She wasn't dressed yet though it was eleven o'clock. Usually she's up at seven. She looked rather odd so I asked her what was the matter. She said: "All morning I've been battling with my husband. He's got a headache and won't get dressed. I'm afraid he'll catch a cold. You've come at the right time, I'm exhausted. Come in and see him and tell him that if he doesn't get dressed he won't have any ideas. Perhaps that'll make up his mind for him. Will you?"

I went into Latirail's bedroom. He was sitting in the middle of the room with only his underpants on.

"What do you want?"

"I've come to say that Sinture is going to . . ."

"Please, don't talk to me about Sinture. Don't mention that turd to me. I've got a headache, I've lost the thread. Don't bother me."

"Listen, Sinture says that when he dedicates your book he'll get his own back on everybody. Couldn't you . . ."

"That's enough. I couldn't care less about Sinture. He's nothing but a self-important nonentity. He's jealous of my novel."

"He knows . . ."

"He knows nothing. Do you think he can help me with my Lice Seekers? Wait, I've an idea . . . I could arrange things so that they find Sinture. Sinture's lice, Sinture's filth. That's right, Sinture is a louse. That's exactly what he is, a louse. Oh, yes! We'll fix him, you'll see . . ."

"It's a bad idea. If you let Sinture get mixed up with your novel you'll never be able to get rid of him. He'll know about it straight away and he'll mess everything up even more. No, you haven't any ideas, or you're just saying the first thing that comes into your head. You can't write like that. These seekers of yours, do you want them to find anything or not? You've got to think ahead. You're not me. When I think ahead I become dumb. But you, with your novel, you've got to know what's going to happen. And you won't do it by picking up just any old idea. What do you want them to find?"

"Treasure. Under a heap of old clothes, one day, in Spain, after travelling throughout Europe in search of different kinds of lice, which they sell to lice trainers, because lice as well as fleas can be trained, they become rich and travel for pleasure and one day, in a market-place, one of them stumbles over a pile of old clothes. He bends down and out of habit pokes around among them and he finds the golden bowl . . ."

"There you are! You knew all along!"

"Perhaps not a market-place, because that would mean that someone had hidden the bowl on purpose. Theft would only complicate matters. In a cave. I can fill in the details later. Anyway, treasure discovered by chance."

"That's a marvellous idea!"

"Yes, but that's only the end. At present, I'm still at the time when they're looking for lice. And I've run out of ideas. I could quite easily make them meet up with Sinture . . ."

"I wouldn't if I were you. Perhaps you've run out of ideas because you've got a headache. Perhaps if you got dressed . . ."

"Do you think so? Ninette has been making a scene all morning . . . She told you to say that, didn't she?"

"No, I thought of it because you don't seem to be on form . . ."

"You never are on form when you've got a headache. Putting on a shirt won't get rid of it."

"Try all the same."

"All right, then . . . I put on my shirt. I button it up. I put on my trousers. I put on my sweater. Satisfied? Well, I feel worse then I did before."

"It'll go. Oh, I've got an idea for your novel! You say that the Lice Seekers . . . What are they called?"

"Fio, Fian and Fion."

"Er, well, Fio, for example, you say how one day he was out walking in Fontoine. Fontoine is where I go for my holidays. He's out walking when suddenly he meets a certain gentleman. This gentleman asks him his name and he replies: 'Fio. And you?' 'My name is Louse. You wouldn't think so, would you? Yes, I'm a real louse. It's a case of transformation. By sucking people's blood I've grown enormous and now I wear a hat and shoes. I'm on holiday here. I itch all over.' Fio is delighted. He'll be able to sell this fat louse to a trainer. He'll fetch a big price. So he asks him: 'Would you like to be trained? You'd be a real attraction. I could find a special trainer. In a circus for example . . .' 'And how would I be paid for these shows?' 'You could ask for a percentage of the takings. Of course, you wouldn't be your own boss, but I'm sure a percentage could be agreed on. What do you say? Is it a deal?' 'All right.' So they catch a tram, which takes them to Agapa-la-Ville. They get off. But Fio has forgotten the way to the circus. He asks a policeman. The policeman says: 'Why do you want to know?' 'We want to find a louse-trainer.' 'But I'm a louse-trainer.' So Fio introduces Louse. The policeman says he's got a good style. Louse thinks he'll pull off a deal. What a stroke of luck—he's always so bored on holiday. And he does pull it off. The policeman buys Louse for one thousand francs. Fio takes the money. He shakes hands with Louse and says: 'Good luck, many thanks, hope to see you again.' He catches the tram back to Fontoine. Fian and Fion are waiting for him at the hotel. He tells them everything that has happened. They look very surprised. And when he has finished his story they say: 'We too have found some big lice. They are ladies who were once lice. They are quite magnificent. We're going to sell them. Here they are!' They open the bathroom door and there they are waiting quietly . . ."

"No, it's no good."

"Why not?"

"Because it's completely crazy. I don't write about crazy

things, I write about real things. God, my head!"

"I really don't understand you. Your head aches because you overwork it. I never have a headache."

6

The Drunks

As soon as Fio had gone, Louse and the policeman burst out laughing. It was all a trick. Louse had been sent by Sinture to meet Fio. And poor Mahu thought he had had an idea! . . . It was Sinture who had given him the idea, in an attempt to introduce this preposterous fellow into Latirail's novel. But Latirail wouldn't have it. Sinture didn't know yet that his attempt had failed. After all, he doesn't know everything.

After having a good laugh and drinking a glass of white wine, Louse and the policeman began to feel ill at ease. How were they going to tell Sinture that Latirail had no use for them? They were at a complete loss and drummed their fingers on the edge of the bar. Their wives expected them back for dinner. Their friends would ask them why they didn't look well. The policeman began to recite the traffic regulations, but kept forgetting what came next. He felt as if he'd commited a crime. He took out his note-book and began to write down a report of the incident. Louse asked him what he was doing and said it was a good idea; he said he'd been thinking about doing so himself. He also wanted to be mentioned in the report, the policeman wasn't the only one to be involved. And they would show the report to Sinture before putting it through the usual channels. This would make it look official, Sinture would realize *de visu* that if the policeman no longer knew the more important traffic regulations by heart it was because of him. He would be responsible for road accidents in the policeman's sector, because a policeman who no longer knew them by heart can cause accidents. He must get the thousand francs he had paid for Louse back from Fio, explain the situation to him and ask to be excused. But what would Fio's reaction be? And, more important, what would happen to Latirail's novel? It was absolutely necessary that Latirail should finish it, so that he,

Sinture, could dedicate it.

Louse and the policeman were somewhat comforted by this idea of the report. They had another glass of white wine. They decked out the report with the addition of drawings and 1 millimetre scales. The exact position of the policeman when Fio came up to him. The exact positions of Fio and Louse. An arrow showed the way to the circus and the policeman emphasised that Fio did not go to the circus. He wondered whether he ought to make a plan of the circus nevertheless. After all, what would have happened if Louse had been taken on by the special trainer? Louse advised him to do so. It would be more precise. They drew a plan of the circus. They began talking about its owner, whom the policeman knew. The policeman had to confess that he was a trainer in his spare time. It would create a bad impression on his superiors, but he put it down in his report. He explained his methods, he related the experiences he had had with lice. He mentioned that his wife, Julia, didn't want to hear anything more about training and that he had quarrelled with his mother-in-law. Not only because of that. They thought he didn't get enough pay increases.

It was then Louse's turn. He wrote down a confession of his transformation and how embarrassing it was. They did their best to be as vague as possible about this. And why he was on holiday in Fontoine. And why he agreed to let Fio take him to Agapa. He declared that he was unmarried. When he said "my wife" he really meant his mistress, to whom he had not yet admitted his real identity: she thought he was just like any other man.

At two o'clock in the morning, they were still in the bar, surrounded by the various parts of the report. The barman had provided them with paper table-cloths. They were bigger, the drawings could be made clearer and explanations could be added.

Louse and the policeman were exhausted. And the barman wanted to go to bed. They had a last glass of white wine. And when they saw all the work they had done they began to feel ill at ease again. They felt smaller from having written so much and weak. They admitted aloud that they were failures. "Barman, take a look, just take a look. All this is our lives. All these papers are us. The préfecture will know everything about us. And all because of that frightful character Sinture. We've failed."

And drunk as they were, they began to cry. They could no longer stand on their feet. The barman pushed them outside. He was surprised to see how light they were. He thought: "They're right, they are failures" and before shutting the door he threw all the pages of the report after them.

When they found themselves out on the pavement, they wanted to die. But one doesn't die like that. One is still a person, even in suspense. What distinguishes the drunks we meet on the pavement? How can we tell one from another? We can't. We don't worry any more, since they've all got shirt collars, sleeves and stains on their trousers just like you and me. No, one doesn't die like that. One spends the night on the pavement like all the other drunks and next day one can't remember anything.

7

The Shampoo

I only write things that are real, thought Latirail. Poor Mahu doesn't understand. Things that are real. In fact, my lice seekers are not very real. They don't ring true somehow. I'll change them to *nails*. I won't have to alter anything. They're looking for old nails that they then sell again. They can still have exactly the same adventures.

I must say something about girls: "Fifteen-year-old girls have greasy hair. When they go to a ball they wash their hair in vinegar. But their partners begin to feel sick, because the vinegar has an unpleasant smell." That's something real. My novel will be filled with such remarks. One should use the material of ordinary life.

Let's look up *nail* in the dictionary. It'll give descriptions, which should give me lots of ideas.

"Ninette! . . . Ninette! . . . Where have you put Larousse?"

"Just a minute, I'm coming . . . Larousse? Let me think now . . . Oh, yes! I lent them to the So-and-sos. But that was six months ago. I forgot all about them. What do you want them for? As book-ends? You could use logs. Wait a minute . . ."

"No, no, I need Larousse. I need them urgently. I can't do without them. How do you expect me to write without Larousse?"

"I didn't know you used Larousse. How've you managed for the past six months, then?"

"That's just it. I haven't been able to think for the past six months. I haven't had any ideas for the past six months. I'm not getting on with my novel . . . Go at once to the So-and-sos."

"What, now? They'll think I'm mad! I can't tell them that you need Larousse for ideas . . ."

"But it's true. Tell them . . . We want information for

example . . . on mushrooms. You bought some mushrooms for dinner and you think they might be poisonous ones. Yes, do that."

"But you can ask the greengrocer that."

"No, no, you don't trust the greengrocer."

"Then why would I have bought the mushrooms from him?"

"Because you only thought about it afterwards when the shops were all shut."

"But I could cook the mushrooms tomorrow . . . They'll think I'm completely crazy to disturb them at nine o'clock in the evening . . ."

"All right, then the mushrooms didn't seem very fresh and so as not to have to throw them away you want to cook them at once."

"Oh, do I? And you think that's worth an hour's journey there and back? You don't think they'll find that rather strange?"

"No, it's plausible."

"Then . . . Oh, what the hell! I'm sick to death of you and your Larousse. I'm hungry. I'm going to get something to eat."

"Ninette, please! I swear to you, it's urgent. Think of me, think of us, think of my nail seekers . . ."

"Your what seekers?"

"Nail seekers."

"Oh, so we've finished with the lice, have we?"

"Yes, it seems more real. I want to write a novel about real things. It must be full of things taken from real life. Listen to this for example: 'Fifteen-year-old girls have greasy hair. When they go to a ball they wash their hair in vinegar. But their partners begin to feel sick because the vingear has an unpleasant smell.' Don't you think there's something real about that, eh?"

"But you don't use vinegar to wash your hair any more! You use shampoo. Didn't you know that? And you a novelist!"

"Oh. Even fifteen-year-old girls?"

"Especially fifteen-year-old girls!"

"Even in the country? I could add '*in the country*' . . ."

"Even there. And in any case they don't have greasy hair any more. Modern hair-setting dries up the hair completely."

"Do you think so?"

"What do you mean, do I think so? What do you look at when you're out walking? And you don't say 'go to a ball', but simply dancing . . . Oh, for heaven's sake, don't start crying! Try and be a bit more up to date, listen to what people say. Then I'll go over what you write."

"All right, then I'll change it to shampoo. That will sound more real."

"And who do you think will be interested . . . And in ten years, well, shampoo . . ."

8

The Larousse

"Good morning, Monsieur Sinture."

"Good morning Mademoiselle Lorpailleur."

"Have you got a letter for me?"

"Yes, Mademoiselle. Here it is."

"Thank you, Monsieur Sinture . . . Er, Monsieur Sinture . . . er, how shall I put it . . . You know I write novels?"

"Oh, do you? First I've heard. Congratulations."

"Oh, you're making fun of me, Monsieur Sinture . . . Yes, it's strange. I just took to it, like that. I can't help it. It's in connection with my work that I've really come. I would like . . . Oh, how shall I put it . . . You know so much . . . I would like some information on Monsieur Latirail."

"Oh, Mademoiselle . . ."

"Yes, Monsieur. You know so much. Perhaps you could tell me what he's writing at the moment?"

"But, Mademoiselle! How would I know? And even if I did, professional secrecy . . ."

"Be careful, Monsieur Sinture, you'll cut yourself . . . We all know you learn a great deal through your job. But I don't blame you. We novelists . . ."

"Mademoiselle, I'm just a simple postman . . ."

"Oh, Monsieur Sinture, tell me something about Monsieur Latirail! I would like to write something about him. I want to know what he's writing at the moment. It's so important for my new novel . . ."

"Just this once, then, Mademoiselle, as a special favour. At the moment, Latirail is writing a story about lice charmers, or something of the kind."

"Has he any ideas?"

"Oh, Mademoiselle . . ."

"Monsieur Sinture!"

"Oh, well, then . . . The answer's no, Mademoiselle. He

hasn't any ideas. He's completely at sea. He's looking up Larousse."

"Is that all?"

"That's all, Mademoiselle."

"Thank you, all the same, Monsieur Sinture. That will give me some ideas. Good-bye, Monsieur Sinture."

"Good-bye, Mademoiselle Lorpailleur."

Sinture rubs his hands with glee. "So he doesn't want my Louse! He wants to go his own way, does he? Well, we'll see!"

"Petite-Fiente, are you there?"—Unless she's already gone home. She was around just now.

"Petite-Fiente!"

"Yes, Monsieur Sinture."

"Catch a tram to Agapa and go to the Café du Cygne. Outside you will find two gentlemen sitting on a bench. A policeman and another gentleman. They're asleep. You will wake them up. The policeman will look at his watch and dash off straightaway. You will say to the other gentleman: 'Are you Monsieur Nail?' And he will reply: 'I think so.' And you will say: 'Yes, you're him. I recognise you. Monsieur Sinture told me to tell you to go immediately to Mademoiselle Lorpailleur's. I'll take you there on the tram.' You understand?"

"Yes, Monsieur Sinture . . . If Papa comes for me, you will tell him where I am?"

"Yes, yes. Hurry up."

Ah, so you want your Larousse, do you? You want the truth? Well, you'll get it. I must write to So-and-so. Pen and paper!

Thursday, 16th.

Dear Sir,

As M. Latirail was here just now, I took the opportunity of asking him if he would lend me his Larousse. He tells me that he lent them to you some time ago.

Would you be so kind as to drop them in for me when you pass the post office at two o'clock? This would be easier for you with your car than for me to collect them from you. As you know, it's almost impossible for me to leave my desk.

I'm depending on you.

Yours faithfully,

Sinture.

If I send it by express it'll get there before twelve. Excellent, excellent.

9

Wrong Ending

A certain Monsieur Nail presents himself at Mlle Lorpailleur's. She doesn't know who he is. He says he has come on behalf of M. Sinture. She telephones Sinture. He says he doesn't know who it is. She rings off. She tells M. Nail that she is very sorry, but she can be of no assistance to him. He leaves.

She returns to her work. She is writing the story of Latirail the novelist. She now knows that he is writing about lice charmers or something of the kind. But she has an original idea. She will transpose it. Instead of writing the life of Latirail she will write the life of a scientist, a seeker. Yes, that's it. A seeker. What of? Never mind that now. That can be decided later. What will he be called, now . . . Nail! Marvellous! *Nail, the Seeker*. Mlle Lorpailleur is overjoyed. She now has a title and a subject. She goes and telephones to her friends. The friends congratulate her. They are proud to be her friend. Especially Julia, the policeman's wife. Mlle Lorpailleur rings her last of all. Julia is dumbfounded. She cannot understand how anyone could have so many ideas. In the end she doesn't know what to say, so she talks about her husband. He spent the night out. He's a drunkard. He'll get thrown out of the police. Mlle Lorpailleur listens. She writes everything down on a note-book. You never know what may come in useful. They will meet for tea next Saturday. "Good-bye, Julia." She rings off. "*Nail, the Seeker*. Incredible!"

Latirail is thinking. For the time being he must give up the idea of the Larousse. The So-and-sos have lent them to someone and they can't remember who. I'll simply have to put myself in the place of one of the seekers and arrange it so that he finds symbolic things. Things that will symbolise my life. For example, a large china bowl will be Ninette. A railway signal will represent my travels. A tube of sleeping pills, my dreams. But what's come over me? I've got so many ideas. Let's say that Fio is the seeker who is me. The two will be simply my assistants. I can't think of discoveries for all three of us. Fian and Fion accompany Fio in his searches. Fian and Fion? No, I don't care for the names. They sound a bit too fantastic. I'll call them . . . Tringla and Boucher. Fio, Tringla and Boucher. No, Bouchez. Pronounced Bouchèze. Why not Bouchèze, then? Fio, Tringla and Bouchèze. Good! *The Nail Seekers*. Original title. At the moment they're in Czecho-Slovakia. Fio is roaming around what used to be a ghetto. That's it, that's it.

Latirail is very pleased with himself. He's made a start at last. He'll not leave his desk. Ninette will end up regretting it. Her husband will have too many ideas. She won't be able to give him advice any more. Suddenly, she'll happen to find the Larousse at Sinture's. She won't suspect anything. She'll put them back in the book-shelves. But by that time her husband will have finished his novel.

Everything will proceed to an end. Mlle Lorpailleur will also have finished her book. She will publish it. Latirail, too, will publish his. *The Nail Seekers* will appear beside *Nail, the Seeker* in the book-shops. People will buy one and read the other. No, people will just glance through it in the book-shops.

10

L'Horizon-Mou

"Guess what, I've just been having an argument with a chap who doesn't think it's possible to write novels. He says you can't put yourself in the place of other people, that Petite-Fiente isn't So-and-so and you're not Mlle Lorpailleur . . . He must be mad. I'm telling you, I could have hit him. He looked at me as if I'd sold him unripe pears. He seemed to think it was my fault. My fault that I didn't understand him! Or rather, that I didn't understand how one couldn't be in a novel. Yes, that was it. That I didn't understand how one couldn't . . ."

"Be quiet, Mahu. Go and see if So-and-so's at home. I've something I want to ask him."

"By the way, look at the paper."

"What? That? The Korean War?"

"No, this: 'IS BOUCHEZE THE MURDERER OF FION?' "

"My God!"

"And this, here: 'A Yugoslav woman was questioned this morning. It appears that Bouchèze was not indifferent to her charms.' What a way of putting it! Must they use periphrases? . . . What's the matter? Are you surprised?"

"No, no. I find it . . . rather curious, that's all."

"You're worried about Fion, eh! He wasn't much use to you, was he? A mere shadow of Fio, as you might say. It's the same with Fian, if he got bumped off . . ."

"Shut up! You disgust me!"

"Oh, so Monsieur's being all sensitive now, is he? As if you didn't know they were all a lot of scoundrels. Who do you think this Bouchèze is? Isn't he one of the same gang?"

"No . . . I don't know. Listen, go to the police station. Try and see the usher or a reporter. Try and find out who Bouchèze is. Get details. Yes, you must. Don't come back . . .

or rather, go to the paper's editorial office. Yes, that's it, go to the editorial office . . ."

"What are you getting so worked up about? Gracious me, that bit of news *has* affected you. Are you afraid for Fio? Isn't what you've read in the paper enough!"

"No. Go on!"

"All right, all right. I'm going."

Latirail reads the rest of the article. Column 4:

This may not be the first action of this kind committed by the criminal. It is thought that the disappearance a little time ago of a certain Fian, probably a relation of Fion, near Le Rouget, is not unconnected with this affair. Bouchèze denies everything.

(continued on p. 10, column 8)

The Statement of Dr Tronc:

Called by the judge to examine the accused, Dr Tronc says in his report, which he considers to be incomplete, owing to the speed with which it had to be made, that Bouchèze is perfectly sane. Yet the psychological tests which he made on the patient, together with certain of his statements, cannot exclude the hypothesis that Bouchèze, on previous unspecifiable occasions, may sometimes have acted in a state of irresponsibility.

The facts: Emile Fion, 45, second-hand dealer, residing at 7, rue des Casse-Tonnelles, Isard, was found strangled, on 12 April last, at his home, on a pile of second-hand clothes and old iron. A paper garrot made of pages of the newspaper *L'Horizon-Mou* lay beside the body of the victim. A neighbour from the same floor of the building, Louis Bouchèze, a second-hand dealer, who was to take over, some days later, the apartment of Fion, who had been forced to leave, has disappeared from Isard. From what the inhabitants of the village have said, the two dates are the same. The police in Isard have found old copies of *L'Horizon-Mou* in Bouchèze's apartment. This case has been delayed in coming to the attention of the public prosecutor's office of this town, because the Isard police saw fit to conduct their inquiries alone for almost two months. The Public Prosecutor intends to order arrests. The said Bouchèze, who was apprehended four days ago at Agapa by Inspectors Boulle and Noirot, will be questioned again tomorrow morning, as will the Yugoslav woman, Nadine Karas, who has also been detained.

II

L'Horizon-Mou
(continued)

SENSATIONAL DECLARATION BY NADINE KARAS:
"I MET BOUCHEZE IN THE METRO."

When questioned this morning, Bouchèze continued to deny that he had committed the crime. He had left home on an unusually long round. He claims to be an expert in the second-hand nail business and, in the course of his work, pays regular visits to the villages around Isard. His declarations have been confirmed by a number of witnesses. As for Nadine Karas, he claims to have never met her. He knew Fion, his neighbour, to whom he sometimes sold part of his stock. The said Fian, who has disappeared from Le Rouget is unknown to him. The accused was even under the impression that the judge was joking when the latter asked him if he knew Fian. This gave rise to some speculation, especially as a witness, M. André Fio, also appeared yesterday before the examining magistrate.

Mlle Nadine Karas, 25, of Yugoslav nationality, had admitted having met Bouchèze in the métro. He claims that she did not pursue this acquaintance. The buying of certain quantities of nails between the 12th and the 27th March was the only result of this meeting. She had asked her friend Traïko to get rid of the merchandise. She has not seen Bouchèze since then.

The examining magistrate has called in two psychiatric specialists to assist Dr Tronc in the new report that he is now preparing.

The accused remains a subject of great interest. He does, in fact, seem to have genuine lapses of memory and, on occasion, to employ in his statements utterly meaningless phrases and interjections, such as: "I, Latirail" or "I writer", which would appear to support—though extreme caution must be exercised in the formulation of such a view—the hypothesis that Bouchèze is not responsible for his actions, even though the murder may subsequently be imputed to him.

The statement of Traïko will be heard by the examining magistrate tomorrow.

TRAIKO, MODEL AT THE BEAUX ARTS:

M. Traïko, 22, appeared before the examining magistrate this morning. The witness remembers having sold, at the request of his friend, several kilos of nails to a foundry, last April. He has no knowledge of Bouchèze. The witness is at present the secretary of Miss Goldwick-Baramine, the well-known millionairess, but had previously worked for two years as a model at the Beaux Arts.

The examining magistrate did not take the matter any further.

Bouchèze's lawyer has requested that his client be freed on bail.

NEW DEVELOPMENTS IN THE BOUCHEZE CASE?

Our readers will recall that this case was temporarily suspended some months ago on account of the internment of Bouchèze in a mental hospital. They will now be surprised to learn that Miss Goldwick-Baramine, whom we mentioned in connection with one of the witnesses, today opened legal proceedings against us. She is suing this newspaper for damages and defamation of character. We feel we are under no obligation to defend ourselves in these columns. The claims made by Miss Goldwick are quite without foundation. Meanwhile, work on the case is proceeding and we shall be returning to it in due course.

12

Who are you?

A Yugoslav woman, full of the charm of her native land, is standing on the platform of a métro station awaiting the arrival of the train. Her charm is tired of being Yugoslav and goes and alights on a paralytic sitting near the exit. The paralytic gets up like you or me. And what does he do? He beats up the Yugoslav woman. Everybody finds it quite charming. The train arrives and the paralytic gets into a carriage. After the second stop he collapses. He becomes a paralytic once more. The people are too closely packed to take any notice. Anyway, the charm has already passed on to someone else. This time, an ugly young woman. Suddenly, she finds all the men looking at her. She thinks she must have omitted to wipe her nose properly, blushes, takes out a mirror from her handbag and sees her charm. She is delighted. At the third station, a gentleman asks her: "Are you getting off here?" She gets off with him. They love each other. He's rich. They go to the Rue de la Paix, he buys her a diamond *rivière* and everybody in the street turns round to look at the girl who has such fabulous charm.

They visit *couturiers*, hairdressers, shoe-makers—the usual build-up, in fact. In the evening, they go to bed together. But at the crucial moment . . . the gentleman turns back. He pretends he has tooth-ache. The girl isn't used to it, she doesn't know what to do. She realises she hasn't a thing on and goes and puts on her night-dress. She looks at herself in the mirror: she's got her old face again.

The charm, in fact, has taken flight into Egypt. It troubles for a moment a family dining out on the terrace. For a brief moment, it alights in turn on the father, the mother and each of the children. The maid who is holding the soup tureen, follows it with marvelling eyes. The charm makes a mistake and drops into the soup. In a split second, the soup tureen is empty and the bellies full. The maid brings in the next course, but they tell her that the soup was stale.

The charm becomes nocturnal in Capri, northern in Norway and Turkish in Sarajevo. It stays longer in Sarajevo. It feels at home there. It goes down to Ragusa, then takes a plane to Spain.

"What a charming steward!" think the lady passengers.

"What charming passengers!" thinks the steward.

"What a charming journey!" say the couples.

"What a charming snack!" say the eaters.

Quite charming, charming, charming, CHARMING. All the engines stop and, plop, the plane drops into the sea.

Girls, be not prodigal of your charms—it may bring disappointment. Travellers, do not say "charming" any more, it is dangerous. Another thing: fear snake-charmers, priests and necromancers. They have power over evil. Be careful to keep your own to yourself. You will never do any good without it; you will lose your taste for living; you will be canonised. And for that to have any charm, a great many processions and religious pictures are required. And how do you know you'll be able to afford them?

13

He who sleeps eats

It's almost time to eat. It's almost time. It's almost time. There! It's time. He's ready to eat. He goes to the grocer's. He takes this and that, pays, goes out again and meets someone who asks him the time.

"It's time to eat."

"What time do you eat."

"I haven't a particular time. And you?"

"No, neither have I. What have you got there?"

"Oh, this and that."

The other man thinks: "Yes, it's time." He goes home.

"What have you got to eat, wife?"

"Spaghetti, as usual. What's the matter with you? What are you pulling a face for? Go and have a look at the prices of things. The So-and-sos only eat every other day. They say one gets used to it. While we can, we'll eat every day; but perhaps we ought to get used to it too."

At the So-and-sos' it is a day without. They don't know what the time is. One of them comes home from the factory, the other from the factory. It's time to sleep.

"What time to you want to sleep till?"

"I don't know. What time is it now?"

"I don't know. Let's just go to sleep. We'll see. We eat tomorrow."

The time says to itself: "I'm going to eat. Let's see. Everybody else is eating. So I'm going to eat too. What are those two doing sleeping? Let's eat them." It does so. It feels quite funny at first. Then it gets used to it. It sets out to look for all the others who are sleeping instead of eating. It finds quite a lot of them. It eats them. One after another. One after another. One after another, one after another, one after another, it can't stop, it's got so used to it, it becomes hysterical. It doesn't know the time any more. It goes off its head. It goes straight for those who are asleep. Instead of waking them to ask them the time, it eats them.

The habit of not eating does the opposite. It takes itself seriously. It considers itself to be a habit. An acquired habit. It slumbers deeply in this habit. It is there wherever anyone is asleep. It is everywhere. It is acquired everywhere. It is caught. It catches on. It takes on. It is taken literally. It takes itself for someone else. It takes to thinking: "If I don't take, I'll be taken. I haven't been taken yet, so I must take all those who haven't taken on the habit yet. We'll see." So it takes all those who are eating. They don't feel anything. They say to themselves, "It's time not to eat", as if one could say to oneself, "It's time not to eat", and not take on the habit. They do take it on. They are taken. They are caught. They sleep.

It's a horrible sight to see.

There used to be two camps, those who ate and those who did not eat. Now there are only those who do not eat and those who are eaten. It's the same thing. The time to eat that eats you while you sleep in order not to eat kills you. The habit of not eating forces you to sleep and you are eaten by the time to sleep, you are dead.

The dead don't eat any more. They have forgotten the time, they float, they remember. They remember that they might have lived. They think of nothing else and the idea goes on killing them for ever—this is eternity.

But what would happen if they suddenly thought of something else? If suddenly they weren't eternal any more? And, no longer being eternal, they wanted to take revenge? Since revenge is all right for the living, afterwards it's all over with, it's eternity.

One might see revenge re-forming the two camps. To warm you up inside a bit. Get drunk. Re-forming the two camps with only those who want to take revenge would mean with everyone, since there'd be no one left to be revenged on. The two camps having been one in the idea of taking revenge would be two to satisfy that revenge, they would be enemies. They would want to kill each other.

But vengeance is long. It passes slowly. They'd have time to be hungry. They'd have time to want to eat.

There would be those who eat and those who do not eat. They wouldn't remember having been in the same eternal mess. Once upon a time.

14

Latirail is stand-offish

Latirail wakes up. He'll get dressed he says to himself. Ninette is away on holiday. He rings. The armchair appears!

"Did Monsieur wish to get up? Monsieur shouldn't. Monsieur hasn't slept. Monsieur should rest."

The chair stands there benignly awaiting his reply. Latirail dismisses it with a pat on the arm. Go back to sleep, he thinks, that's just what I mustn't do. Mustn't be like people who go back to sleep. Not original. Is it original to get up, if it comes to that? Suppose not.

Quite by chance, he rings again, to give himself time to think. In comes the rain of the day before. It drenches the blankets. It floods the room. It gets into everything.

"A little walk in the rain, perhaps? You'll get very hot today. Benefit from the rain while you can. No one can do without a little rain."

He absolutely refuses to get up in such circumstances. He'd be no better off than a drowned man.

The rain goes. Latirail is beginning to feel ill. He has understood the trick now. Every time he rings it'll be the same. He thinks of ringing for himself. He presses his right nipple.

"Hello, yes? Who is speaking?"

"Latirail here. I'd like to get up."

"Latirail? Don't know him."

"What? It's me, me, you understand?"

They've rung off. He tries his left nipple:

"May I come in? Sorry, I mean, can you come in? I want to get up."

"Well, get up then!"

"What I mean is, I'm a little worried about my originality. Would it, in your opinion, be original? I'd be very much obliged if you . . ."

"Strange, I was about to ask you the same thing. So, as you mention it, I might as well ask you . . ."

"What do you mean, you too? . . . That's a bit much . . . By the way, to whom have I the honour? . . ."

"Latirail."

"What?"

"L, A as in LA, T, I as in TI . . ."

This time, he rings off. He then gets up. He shaves. He has his coffee. Very depressing. Everyone's in the same state. He tries to laugh it off, defiantly. And in doing so he becomes even more like everyone else. He puts his right foot into his right sock and his left foot into his left sock; he puts on his braces; he buttons up his flies; he takes out a clean handkerchief; he double-locks his door; he doesn't say good morning to his concierge. Outside, he says: "Good God, what weather!" It is raining. He takes advantage of the fact to perform his little experiment. When the rain is very heavy, it forms a mirror and you can see yourself on all sides. It's very pleasant for the back and the profile. When he raises his foot, three million feet rise with it. When he scratches his ear, three million hands scratch three million ears. They are my hands, my feet. Or rather my hand, my foot. Oh, look, I've put my jacket on inside out. Inside out? Yes, north, south, east and west, three million jackets inside out. Latirail stops. The jackets continue on their way. My God, what's happening? The other one moves on. It's me that's moving. Hey, wait, I'm just coming!"

He bumps into a gentleman.

"Oh, excuse me, I thought it was me . . ."

The gentleman looks very surprised.

Damn, it didn't work, thinks Latirail. First time I took myself for someone else.

The gentleman has walked on. He is thinking exactly the same thing. He too was performing an experiment and he bumped into Latirail. He is very annoyed. He thought it was an original experiment. So he invents another one and bumps into Latirail again:

"This time, Monsieur, would you please put your jacket on right side out. It's been annoying me a great deal."

"But, Monsieur . . ."

It wasn't Latirail any more. It was someone else. Latirail was standing off, observing the scene with some concern.

15

Latirail travels

I loathe journeys, thinks Latirail. I'm worried sick before them, I'm sick with fever during them and I come back feeling thoroughly depressed. I don't get *that* out of them.

If I am making another, it is because of Ninette. She wants a change, as she says. Personally, I never feel any different after them, on the contrary. I leave her to her illusions. Who knows? She may change her mind one day. We've been discussing our next journey. Or rather, I let her talk, contenting myself with remarks such as "Do you think we'll have time?" or "Wouldn't it be too dear", just to show that I'm listening, but I get so bored with these discussions . . . She's well aware of this. She calls me Dear Time when she's making plans, but she goes on just the same. She thinks it keeps me up to the mark. She thinks that if she wasn't there my brain would atrophy altogether. I let her talk. We're going . . .

I must admit that the reason why I give in to Ninette so much is because of a prophecy. A fortune-teller predicted that I would go on many journeys. And I can't go against that, can I? It gives me an opportunity to test whether it is true. Unfortunately, I have a niggling doubt. Don't fortune-tellers often predict a great many journeys?

So we leave. I'm feverish as soon as the journey begins. It may seem contradictory, but that's how it is, I catch my fever from her or rather I have her fever. She, of course, comes to life. She enjoys herself tremendously. I get more and more feverish, until I can't see or think any more. I'm as sick as a dog. Ninette sits beside me, wallowing in sympathy. It's quite intolerable. To pass the time, I write to various acquaintances. At the bottom of the page, I always write: "N.B. Please return this letter to my home address." When we get back, I find a whole pile of letters. I read over them and correct them—that takes quite a lot of time. And they're so boring . . . Then I tie them all up together and mark the parcel: "Journey to X", "Journey to Y" etc. I could weep when I see the new pile of letters next to the old ones. My piles of journeys! They are on the top shelf of the book-shelves. They are yellowing with age.

When will Ninette change her mind? I told her that she didn't gain anything from travelling either. It's broadened her mind so much she's lost all sense of discrimination. She meets people. They're friends because we met them while travelling. The greater their mileage, the better they are. She invites them round. We're on Christian-name terms straightaway—it's more informal. But I don't know what to talk to them about. When they've gone, Ninette makes a scene because I didn't slap them on the back and because I looked as if I was bored to death. I do try and get something out of travelling. I speak to anybody on the road, in hotels, in stations. The first chap I had a drink with talked to me about his wives. The first woman I bought a newspaper off talked to me about her marriage. Ninette says it is human contact.

16

Latirail Burns

I was in our room day-dreaming. It must have been about seven o'clock in the evening. I was smoking. Smoking spoils my appetite. Ninette was sitting in the armchair. She smelt of celery. She had been making soup.

We were waiting for it to cook. I was blinking because of the smoke. When I smoke while day-dreaming it gets in my eyes. In the half-light I could see behind the book-shelves. My wife put the light on. The shade is burnt on one side and you can see the bulb. The book-shelves faced the burnt side. I saw all my journeys yellowing on the top shelf. Even the last one didn't look new any more.

My wife got up. It was the end of the month and she had to prepare the potato salad. We usually make do with potato salad during the last few days of the month. As she went by I caught a whiff of celery.

I climbed on to a chair. I took down all my piles of letters. My hands were black—it never gets dusted up there. I untied them and threw them in bundles of five or six into the stove.

I sat down again. My Gauloise had gone out. Ninette came back.

"There's a smell of burning paper."

"There may well be. I've just burnt the journeys."

"What? Burnt the journeys? All of them? What came over you?"

"I don't know. I've burnt everything."

"You must be mad. What will we do now?"

"Oh, it's not very important. They were only old letters after all. We never looked at them. It got on my nerves thinking of those journeys in all those letters."

"So it's all finished with. We never did anything at all? We just sat like dummies in this room?"

"You're crazy. Of course we made the journeys. We've got them in our heads. You can think about them whenever you like. We remember them."

"We remember them, do we? Then tell me all about the journey to Fontoine."

"Well, we set off . . . Let me see, what day *was* it?"

"You see!"

"It doesn't matter. We arrived at . . . What do you call that . . ."

"You see!"

"We went walking for a fortnight."

"What then? Very interesting! You see, you can't remember. A lot of good you are! How are you going to tell the So-and-sos all about it, now you haven't got the letters? What are we going to say to them?"

"Damn, that's true. What are we going to say to them?" Can't you remember?"

"Who? Me? You know me."

"Damnation, what came over me? What came over me? Why did you go out?"

"To make the salad."

"To think that I had them there, in my own hands . . . Do you think Mahu will remember? Almost all the letters were addressed to him. To think they were there . . ."

"Go and ring Mahu."

I went and telephoned. He was at the café and Marie went to fetch him from his room. He came to the telephone. I explained to him what had happened. "I'll come right away," he said.

He came. His first words were: "It's a powerful drama." I glanced at my wife. She doesn't like Mahu. She says he makes phrases up, it's just that on sad occasions he repeats phrases he has read in the papers.

17

Melchior

"Still having trouble?"

"It's terrible, old chap. I have lots of ideas, I write them down but I can't do anything with them. It's this Bouchèze. You know he's been let out? It's a catastrophe! Yes, he's left the asylum. The trial didn't take place. The case has been closed. I'm responsible for Fion's murder. Bouchèze is living proof of that. I'm arrested whenever I write his name. I have to say 'he' and when I read over what I've written I don't understand a thing. Look, I've written a hundred pages since the other day, a hundred pages with 'he' mixed up with Fio and Tringla. It's incomprehensible."

"I told you, change his name. It's quite simple, you can make up any name you like. I've thought of some marvellous ones, for example 'Melchior of Sassanasis'. He's an aristocrat who has fallen on hard times and is working with Fio and Tringla. You could recount the whole of Melchior's life up to his ruin. He was born of an old Byzantine family in a castle in Persia . . ."

"I'm not changing anything again. No thank you! Anyway, I've got some ideas. If only I didn't have to write *Bouchèze* . . ."

"Explain, then."

"Explain what?"

"Explain what has happened. You'll feel the better for it. Bouchèze used to be called Fion and you changed his name. Result: Fion was murdered. It won't be held against you. People will understand . . ."

"And what about the police? You don't know the cops. It could go on for years."

"So what?"

"So nothing. Either I go on writing about the adventures of Fio, Tringla and Bouchèze by saying 'he'—and produce a load of gibberish—or I stop writing altogether. There would have been one solution: if Bouchèze had been found guilty. But there's nothing I can do in court. They'd simply ask me what I had to do with the case and that would let the cat out of the bag. If only Bouchèze would change his own name! But one can't depend on him. As it is, he couldn't care less about my novel or me. He doesn't even know who I am. No, the whole thing's ruined."

"What duffers we are! All you have to do is call him 'He' with a capital 'H' . . . Yes, that's it! Then you'll know that 'He' is always Bouchèze and everything will be just as before!"

"My dear chap . . . But . . . that's a marvellous idea! Quite marvellous! You've saved my life!"

"You mustn't let problems like this get you down. Just put one name in place of another. After all, what's in a name? There's no need to lose sleep over it. In a crowd, if you think of all the ideas in the heads of all those people, you're lost, but if you choose one idea, it doesn't matter what it is, or one word, it's enough, everyone will understand it. Like magic. I've experienced it myself. For example, I often amuse myself by making the sound 'ggh', with my tongue; if I try and find out where that sound comes from, I discover it's simply a bottle being uncorked. I didn't invent it at all, it belongs to everyone, anyone can make it, that is to say the totality of the crowd that hears it is nothing more than the sound of a cork coming out of a bottle or any other sound or any word said by anyone, and if you decide that everyone is thinking about it, well, it proves that you have the right to choose . . ."

But Latirail is too happy to be able to write 'He' without lying. He didn't take any notice of what he'd been told. He shook hands with Mahu, who took his leave, and outside, in the Carrefour des Oublies, met a stranger who was just passing through, a very talkative stranger, who, during the hundred yards or so that they walked together, found time to recount his whole life: he was fifty years old, born in Persia, completely ruined and was called Melchior of Sassanasis.

Mahu invited him for a drink at the Café du Cygne.

18

Let's go back to Fontoine

"Let's go back to Fontoine," says Mlle Lorpailleur. "I've taken on *Nail, the Seeker* and I must really get to know Latirail's life, his friends, the places he goes to and so on. You can't transpose something you don't know at first-hand." She jumped on to her Vespa and off she went. She never said "the Vespa rides like velvet," for she is regarded as being rather sporty, something of a dare-devil even, and revels in it. But the Vespa is more than velvet, it's goose-down. And she knows it.

She arrives at Fontoine. She parks the Vespa. Her eye is caught at once by a shop-window filled with all kinds of clothes, men's and women's. She compares the prices with those at Agapa. There are one or two bargains, that twin-set, for example. She looks inside the shop and recognises Mahu, who is trying on a shirt. She goes in. She goes up and shakes hands with Mahu, who is ill at ease in the blue-striped shirt which is much too smart for him.

"Am I disturbing you?"

"No, on the contrary. Would you help me to do up the collar?"

"What size do you take?"

"In five years."

She doesn't understand. He explains that as he is thirty-three years old he adds five and that makes thirty-eight, which is his size. Mlle Lorpailleur considers this to be a bad mnemonic system because next year he'll have to remember to add only four years. Mahu stops:

"That's true, I hadn't thought of that."

He deduces that that was why his previous shirts never fitted him. If this one does fit, it's because he thought to try it on first.

"No, Mahu! It's simply because you're at exactly the right

age to add five and make thirty-eight!"

"This may be. But, anyway, I still don't understand. The main thing is that this shirt fits, and one doesn't buy a shirt that fits every day, in fact it's very seldom one does."

Mlle Lorpailleur helps him to take it off and says that she'll buy it for him. Mahu flings his arms around her neck and thanks her. The assistant who is not used to townspeople is shocked and asks Mlle Lorpailleur, "Shall I wrap it up?"

They then go and have an ice-cream on the terrace of the cake-shop, a very good little cake-shop, where the assistant, who is the baker's daughter, hobbles slightly.

"Do you know," says Mahu, "when she picks you out a cream puff it goes up and down like waves all the way to your plate. It makes a pretty effect."

"Are you staying in Fontoine, Mahu?"

"Yes, for a week's holiday. I find this ice-cream rather cold, don't you?"

"No, I'm always too hot, it's my nature. By the way, where does Latirail stay when he comes to Fontoine?"

"He never comes here, Mademoiselle."

"What? Never? Well, what could have given me that idea? Are you sure?"

"Absolutely, Mademoiselle. Why, would you like him to come? . . . Oh! Look at the milkman's horses, Mademoiselle! How funny they are with their tails rolled up into a bun! Real bum buns! It makes a pretty effect, don't you think?"

"Be serious, Mahu. You seem to be making fun of me."

"Oh, Mademoiselle, how could I? After that shirt you bought me . . . You're really too kind."

"I do my best . . . Well, I haven't got very far with my researches, have I. It strikes me that everything concerning Latirail is rather elusive . . ."

"Not at all, Mademoiselle. Would you like me to introduce you? You could interview him."

"No, no, that's the last thing I want to do, Mahu. That would ruin everything. He mustn't know that I'm writing about him."

"Why not?"

"For the sake of verisimilitude."

"You're talking just like Latirail. He's always on about things being real and true, about veritability or verisimilitude . . . He's got a thing about it."

19

The Truth

"I had to leave the hall and lie down on the pavement. That put my ears back into place. Just at that moment I saw Mlle Lorpailleur arrive. She was coming to the lecture. I said to her: 'Don't go in. It's terribly hot. I nearly fainted.' She was only too pleased to sit down on the pavement beside me. She was tired. She told me all about her life. I couldn't get over it, it was so sad. People think she's a blue-stocking and rather difficult to deal with, don't they? Well, in the first place, she's never written a novel, it's a lie. She attends lectures at the University. She was on the point of getting married and something went wrong. It was her last hope. I know that with some girls sex is the cause of all the trouble. But with Mlle Lorpailleur . . . I just couldn't bring myself to mention it. It wouldn't have seemed in very good taste somehow. You see how wrong one can be about people?"

"My poor dear fellow, you believe anything you're told. She just put on the Children of Mary act just to see what your reaction would be. I still won't give up the idea that she writes. Women can be very clever sometimes, especially that sort. They sometimes find out the most extraordinary things —by their own crooked means."

"Oh? Do you think so? Well, you know more about it than I do . . . Anyway, I've noticed that one often jumps to conclusions about people. Sometimes it's much more complicated, sometimes much simpler. For example, I saw a friend of mine just now who's on leave from the army. He was just catching the train back to camp. And do you know what he talked to me about? Moth-balls. He had forgotten to buy some moth-balls for his civilian clothes and they were all moth-eaten. He left me his key so that I could go and put some moth-balls in his wardrobe.

20

Stories

A friend of mine told me a story about a commercial traveller in the Niger who had asked a negro to try his small medium and large tins of sardines. The negro was wearing a boo-boo, which are a sort of trousers, and apologised for the way he was dressed. He owned a grocer's shop and he would like to taste the sardines straight away. He had two assistants who ate all the sardines. The negro ordered two million tins, but as he could not pay for them, the commercial traveller refused to accept the order. Nevertheless, the negro invited him to dinner. The whole family were wearing boo-boos. They ate dried fish that you rub into the palm of your hand and then bite.

Another story I heard in a bistro. One chap said to another: "Do you know what the priest told us? I remember, it was during the catechism class. He said it was forbidden to hunt on All Saints' Day. And he said it again in church on the Sunday before All Saints' Day; and if the men weren't in church by the beginning of the sermon, he said it at the end. We were still only kids and didn't take any notice. But the men did, and they didn't go hunting. They weren't very pleased about it, because, after all, what can you do on a Sunday? And All Saints' Day is the same as a Sunday. The priest said that if we did go hunting we'd never see either the animals or the dogs again."

I like people to tell me stories. If they didn't, how would I ever know anything? What would happen if suddenly Latirail and the others didn't speak to me any more, or if I became deaf? I must remember to thank them very much when they tell me things. But it's difficult repeating them to other people afterwards. I really ought to have the people who first told me the stories there at the time. But it would be a very difficult matter to arrange for them all to be there on hand as and when required. Supposing I tried to? At least people wouldn't say that it was silly and that it was all my fault.

I really don't know what people expect me to tell them.

21

The Cheque

A dog presented himself at the convent of St Fiducia and asked the holy nun to pray that his master might find him again. His master had lost him one day while hunting and no one had heard anything of him since. But he had continued to prowl around until he hit upon this idea of prayers.

The nun showed him into the parlour. A few minutes later, she returned to say that the Mother Superior would not hear of prayers for dogs. There was no point in insisting. The last time they broke the rule in a matter of this kind was for a goat. And the most dreadful results ensued. They would find the goat at every turn kneeling down in various pious attitudes. It was really most unbecoming. People even began to think that he was St Fiducia herself, who, as everyone knows, appears quite often.

At these words the dog began to blush a deeper and deeper red. The nun asked him what was the matter. And he admitted, naive as he was, that he had long been that very same goat. That there was nothing he could do about it and had hoped in the form of a goat to find his master more easily. "My master lost me while hunting on All Saint's Day."

The nun asked him to sit down. She asked him if he would like a cup of tea. She asked him if he knew anything about St Fiducia.

"Well, er . . . I think we were in touch . . ."

"In touch with the saint? Directly?"

"No, not directly. I would hear sort of calls. Perhaps you'll understand more easily what I mean if I call them tastes of sugar. It's the easiest way of calling a dog. Immediately I turned myself into a goat in order to preserve my incognito. I then felt a taste of salt and set off in search of my master. The most annoying thing of all was these apparitions. I was obliged to behave in a miraculous fashion before the people. The first time I heard of St Fiducia was when people began to beg me to do various things in her name. I cursed the saint . . ."

"Oh! That was a very wicked thing to do! You interceded with Our Blessed Lord! Did you see him?"

"Who?"

"Our Blessed Lord."

"No, Sister, you see . . ."

"But you could have done, since you interceded . . . Yes, yes, you were the instrument by which St Fiducia . . . Then it wasn't a case of scandal at all! We thought the goat was blaspheming! And all the time he was none other than the envoy of our Saint. Oh, Monsieur! Yes, you say you heard calls?"

"Yes, Sister."

"It was our novena! The Saint was answering our prayers! Oh, Monsieur! Let us go and tell our Mother Superior at once! Praise be to God!"

"Excuse me, Sister . . . But may I ask why you made a novena for this goat?"

"Oh, it's a long story . . . All about a goat that was sterile. We'd been begged to pray for her. We refused for a long time. And then, at last, we gave in . . ."

"Then what happened?"

"Then the goat began his apparitions. So we stopped our prayers at once. But the damage was already done . . . But it wasn't a sin at all! You were the miraculous goat! It was you, wasn't it? You say you heard calls? Tell me about them, Monsieur, tell me about them again!"

"Yes, Sister, I heard calls . . ."

"So our Saint, going far beyond your sterility, applied the merits of our novena . . ."

"But it wasn't I who was sterile, Sister. I was a mere response . . ."

"The merits of our novena had some higher purpose, a purpose as yet unknown to us! Dear Lord, what could that purpose be? You see, Monsieur, Our Lord authorised the appearance of scandal, but only the appearance! . . . But to what purpose? Our Mother Superior will know! Come along with me, Monsieur!"

"But that won't help me find my master again, will it? If you're not willing . . ."

"But this changes everything! Everything! Our Mother will certainly agree when she knows!"

The nun took her companion to see the Mother Superior, who found it all very edifying. She said she would have to think about it. Meanwhile, she gave the dog a cheque for three novenas. He thanked her politely and took leave of the poor women.

He passed through the convent gates. He felt very sad and sickened. He was sorry he'd ever called at the convent in the first place. He nearly tore up the cheque, but a slight fear stopped him doing so. He stuck it under his collar and went on his way.

22

Paper

I bought some paper at the National Provincial Paper Company. Am I now a member of this company? I think I must be since I've got a bill. I had to wait a long time for it. The clerk explained that customers who pay in cash have to wait for the bill to go through the accounts department. It's a very complicated business: there are checks, double-checks, stamp duty, percentages. When there are a lot of customers paying cash it takes a very long time. Beside me, on the seat, was a lady with her little boy. She had come to show some samples of material to one of the typists. The typist came and they talked about it in front of me. Perhaps my presence embarrassed them . . . But there was only one seat. The typist chose some frightful material. I wanted to tell her, but I was going to join the company. I was waiting for my bill. Other customers came and asked for paper. The clerk was called to the telephone by another typist; he shouted back that he couldn't take the call because he had a customer. The customer joked and said: "Tell her to say you're on the pot." The clerk then shouted at least five or six times that he was on the pot, on the pot. I thought it was funny but I didn't laugh. The clerk is in a position to make jokes of that kind, he doesn't belong to the company. Unless, of course, he has bills made out for him. Does he buy paper here? I dare say he gets it free. I should think employees get it free. So they don't have bills. And what about the company boss? Same thing. He doesn't have his name in the accounts department.

"Are you talking to yourself?"

"No, no. I was thinking. Would you say that when you curse something, you can do without it?"

"How do you mean, do without it?"

"Well, I've noticed that when people curse or make fun of

people, it's because they can't do without them."

"For example?"

"For example . . . You say 'Blasted stomach!' or 'Bloody glasses'—it's because you can't do without them. If you hadn't got a stomach and glasses you couldn't think of saying it."

"Why talk to me about it?"

"I don't know. I just thought of it. I thought of it because Sinture is always saying: 'Go and hang yourself with your letters!' He made me realise that he couldn't do without them. And there are people who say, 'Your explanations are just a lot of eye-wash.' Well, it's the same thing. They haven't any explanations of their own and can't do without ours. If someone has really invented something, he doesn't spend his whole time comparing it with others' inventions, because his invention has replaced all the others. But if he's always puffing his own goods and running down other inventions, it's because he still hasn't discovered anything. I thought about it because . . . Don't you agree?"

"Me? Oh, I stick to my novel, you know . . ."

"Yes, that's true. It has replaced everything else for you. You've found . . ."

"Unfortunately, that's just it. I haven't! I've just been cudgelling my brains trying to remember who told me about the convent of St Fiducia. It wasn't you by any chance, was it?"

"No. Where is it?"

"It's of no importance. But it's annoying when you forget who told you what."

"That's true. Especially when they're dead. You remember my cousin who we met holding a paper?"

"Yes, what about him?"

"Well, I can't remember whether it was he who talked to me about the resurrection. I had another cousin who is also dead. I never saw him again. I'm sure to bump into him soon because I was trying to remember whether it was he talked to me about it. And I won't dare to ask him because it would look as if I was doubting his existence."

"Why?"

"Because it was he who talked to me about the resurrection. Rather as if he couldn't do without it. Not as much as if he'd cursed it in some way of course. But all the same . . ."

"Well, yes?"

"Well, if he can't quite do without it, it's almost as if he's been resurrected. I wouldn't like to mention it for fear of putting my foot in it. But I'm sure to meet him before long. We'll have to talk about something else . . ."

23

Shorthand,
Sound-photographs

"Do you think it's true what she says? It seems everyone's trying to get a job as a stenographer. The only thing that matters these days is shorthand. She can't understand why I'm not going in for it. Everything will be written down in shorthand. The alphabet, which is as out of date as the Romans, won't be needed any more. Do you realise what that will mean? She'll buy everything in shorthand. She'll simply hand in her list to the shopkeeper, who'd much rather it was done that way than have to listen to her muttering 'One kilo of sugar, two lemons, some pasta in such and such a shape, some vinegar with such and such a flavour, some polish that's not too yellow' and so on. The shopkeeper will simply read the list and put the goods into a shorthand bag. That's what she says, anyway. Do you think it's possible? Wouldn't it be easier just to speak?"

"Oh, she's crazy, I'm telling you. Don't listen to her when she talks like that. By the way, come and have a look at this alphabet. I've just bought it. It's an Albert Dürer. Isn't it beautiful? Look at that A."

"Oh, did he make an alphabet, then? It must have been a kind of shorthand. Yes, that's it, a kind of alphabet of his own, not the alphabet that's as out of date as the Romans . . . You can make the letters as you like. Personally, I'd use it for sounds. At night I hear sounds, but I can never remember them afterwards. Now, if I had a shorthand . . . Sounds. I've tried with my flute—it's called Pan-Pan. But I haven't managed to make them, it's not like music, it's more like *sotto voce*. They come one by one. I sit up in bed, I listen, you mustn't put the light on. They brush past me. Like cats. Softly. I can count them, but they aren't always the same ones. I want to stroke them. It's silly, a sound isn't a cat.

Now, with shorthand! It would be marvellous. You'd hear whatever sounds you wanted. Of course, there are some I don't care for. Where can you learn shorthand?"

"Listen, Mahu, don't talk to me about that again. Do you hear? If your little friend is out of her mind, you shouldn't listen to her. Tell her to leave you alone. I'll have a word with her myself. What's her name, now?"

"Caroline, I think. What's the matter, Caroline's a name. I can't catch her out. She's always calling me an idiot. But I don't mind. She's there at night and that's the main thing. I said to her, 'Caroline, let's learn shorthand.' Do you realise what it means? Do you realise what it'll be like when we don't need sleep any more? We went to the cinema. I lost my ticket before entering the auditorium. I found it, then lost it again before handing it to the attendant. So I went back to the box-office. I'd dropped it. There were two tickets on the ground. I picked them up. The attendant gave me two seats for myself and one for Caroline—she hadn't lost hers. During the whole film she told me a story about a mountain that had just sprung up in her district. It was a very good story. It seems people are already using it for skiing. There's a refreshment-bar at the top from which you can see the Pantheon. It's a real shorthand snow-ball. We're going to learn it by heart. She's agreed."

"Agreed?"

"Yes, in principle. We're going to specialise. It will be our work. You mustn't make fun of us, you wouldn't understand. You're in the habit of supposing things, I know. Well, it's a bad habit in my opinion. You don't know what people are thinking. For example, what am I thinking about now?"

"Shorthand."

"Yes and no . . . Not quite. I'm thinking about my Kodak. I have an old Kodak. I keep it beside my bed. At night, when I hear a sound, I press the lever, click. It takes photographs that are completely dark."

24

Christmas

I met my mother in the street and she said: "Mahu, why don't you come and stay at home for a few days. We'll have a nice roast and a good pudding to fill you out. You're looking old. What would you like for pudding? An apple-charlotte?" So I said all right, just for one day, and I went. Everything was laid out on the table. I'd have liked to have dined outside on the lawn in front of the house, but there was frost on the ground and we had to go inside. I was very careful not to let the doors be shut behind me.

Father was coughing in the kitchen. He was cooking the roast, it was Christmas geese, I said hello how are you, but he didn't answer. I'm very fond of goose. We went to Midnight Mass. It was very restful. In fact, I think the priest was trying to send us to sleep so that he could then lock us up in the church. Marion, who was in the same catechism class as me, was sitting just in front of me. She wears make-up. It seems she's something of a tart. She went to have a look at the crib on the left during the communion and I slipped out to have a look at the geese. We ate the geese with my brothers, who are all married. There are a lot of us when we're all together. Everybody said: "You're thinner, how are you getting on with your parcels?" One of my cousins, who is very good at maths, explained what my chances were. It seems that I must carry twice as many parcels in order to lose two. Usually I lose two out of eight. I'll have to carry at least thirty, it's the law of great numbers. He's got a child who's always saying, "Nine out of ten, nine out of ten." The parents are very pleased, he'll be good at maths.

I had a bad attack of tooth-ache and I had to stay more than a day. I was given aspirins to take and Mother said that I was not to be woken, just as she used to. I was so afraid. The doors began to be locked again. So I took off all the locks in the hotel. Frédy who is making a hen-house at the back of the hotel, puts on a pair of corduroy trousers when he gets back from the office. He's also got a child who doesn't say nine out of ten, fortunately, I hate maths. This hen-house is very modern. It's collapsible, in walnut veneer and has a one-way system for hens that have laid.

I brought presents for everyone. I gave them my best sound-photographs, but I don't think they liked them very much. I saw my photographs left around the bedrooms. I was quite hurt. It's difficult of course. They have a lot of work in their offices and they haven't time to listen to them. Next time I'll have my teeth taken out and they won't be able to say, "Stay for a while."

Every evening Mother says, "What would you like for dinner? I want to see you fill out a bit." One day I didn't know what to say, so I made something up, I said, "Chernel, it's a cross between chervil and fennel," we had a good laugh, and "Turdock, it's a cross between turkey and haddock." It all goes to prove that when I eat I don't have any ideas. And for dessert, "Strawapples, they're a cross between strawberries and pineapples." We got on to discussing food and Frédy told us how one day long ago his mother-in-law came back from the market and meeting her brother-in-law said, "Here's a Camembert for your father, Edmond. I know he likes a bit of Camembert. Here, you can have it." Unfortunately, she'd forgotten that her brother-in-law's father had just died—it was quite macabre.

They're really very kind to me. They ask me out for drives in their cars. They all have cars now and they pretend not to notice my old trousers—it's very tactful of them. I saw their children who have electric trains and little fur coats. They can talk already and they say, "Good morning, Monsieur," then their parents say, "You silly great thing you, it's Mahu. Look! Your Uncle Mahu" and add, tactfully, "They're always talking about you."

They've given me my old room back. It's used as a box-room. It'll do very well for a few days. Before going to sleep, I can hear Father coughing in his room. It's as if he wanted to tell me something from far off, after all, what can he tell me with all those children around, he's a grandfather now and he doesn't know what advice he ought to give a son who carries parcels.

But I like the bathroom best. I have a bath and wash myself with a big sponge, I'm given a clean shirt for Christmas and I drink milk. They have a lot of milk.

25

Waifs and Strays

Mme Julia goes and books some seats for the theatre. She asks for two stalls. She is given seats D14 and 15. She is about to leave when the woman at the box-office calls her back. She is very sorry, she has just checked up on the bookings and must ask Mme Julia her name.

"That's just what I thought. I can't give you D14 and 15."

"Why not?"

"Because you'd be sitting next to Juan Simon. That would never do."

"Who is he, anyway? And why wouldn't it do?"

"Because you don't belong to the same spiritual zone."

Julia is shocked. She says she'll complain to the management. The booking-clerk says she will have to cross the t's and dot the i's. She reveals to Julia the purely episodic nature of her existence. She's nothing but a character invented by M. Mahu, the friend of the novelist Latirail. Julia protests. She says she knows Latirail through her friend Mlle Lorpailleur who happens to be writing a book about him. "So you see." But the booking-clerk doesn't give up so easily. She says that if Julia knows Mlle Lorpailleur it's because of the inexplicable play of chance; that she imagines she knows M. Latirail because her friend has talked to her about him, but doesn't really know him at all; she has never seen him, she has never met him. Such a thing would be quite impossible, because of the zones. That's why it wouldn't do for her to sit next to Juan Simon, it's exactly the same thing.

Julia feels quite humiliated. She doesn't insist on keeping D14 and 15, but, "Since you've raised the matter, could you tell me what would have happened? The clerk says she doesn't know, it's just unthinkable. She gives Julia seats J25 and 26. Julia then asks, "What about the actors? They'll be in my zone, won't they?" The booking-clerk bursts into laughter and reassures her that they will. "There could be no question of them not being, Madame."

Julia leaves the theatre with her tickets. She has still got a little shopping to do before lunch. Among other things, she must enquire as to the price of a vacuum-cleaner. Her husband says he will buy her one for Christmas, there's a lot he should feel sorry about. But Julia is afraid it might cost too much. She enters the first vacuum-cleaner shop she sees. She is given information and shown all the different models. She is particularly intrigued by one machine.

"That's not a vacuum-cleaner, Madame," says the young man, "it's an F.S. detector."

"What's that?"

"A false-security detector. You just plug it in like any other machine."

"Is it expensive?"

"Oh, Madame, it's good enough for the Aga Khan."

Julia asks the price of a hair-drier and leaves the shop. She hasn't had time to do half her shopping and it's already half-past twelve. Her husband who has to be back at the police station by a quarter-past one is getting very impatient. She quickly fries some eggs and opens a tin of sardines. She says "Don't forget we're going to the theatre this evening. Try and be back by half-past seven." He says he'll try.

In the evening they go to the theatre. It's the first time they've been in the stalls. The policeman insisted that Julia should get stalls, again because of all the things he should feel sorry for. She is wearing her blue dress and he his blue suit. When he's in civilian clothes, he could be taken for a civilian. He's wearing a tie with Donald Duck embroidered on it. J25–26 are good seats. "Let's look out for this Juan Simon and his wife next to D14 and 15," says Julia. It's just in front of the pillar, I noticed it on the plan. No one else has arrived yet. They look at the ceiling, at the gilt. The policeman shows Julia where the emergency exit is, you never know. Julia points out to her husband a woman painted on the ceiling who has a large stain on her belly. She remembers that she forgot to wash her husband's pyjamas. "You should have reminded me."

Ah! The people placed next to those in seats D14 and 15 have come in. So they must be the Juan Simons. Julia thinks they look vulgar. The policeman thinks he knows them. "No," says Julia "You couldn't possibly. They don't belong to the same zone." Seats D14 and 15 remain empty. It's now nine o'clock. The show will begin at any moment. An attendant comes up to the policeman and asks to see his tickets.

"You see, Mademoiselle, J25 and 26!"

"There's been a mistake, Monsieur. Your seats should be D14 and 15."

They have no time to explain. The attendant moves them quickly to their new seats. The curtain rises. A young woman is sitting at a Louis Quinze *secrétaire*. She is writing a letter. She does not notice a servant coming up behind her. He gets closer and closer . . . and grrr he strangles her with a kind of paper garrot. The young woman falls to the ground. The servant cries: "Long live Latirail! Lorpailleur is dead!"

Julia is struck speechless. In the second act, the plot is complicated by the question of an inheritance. Heirs who are not suspected arrive. They suspect other heirs who are absent. The third act is absurd. The notary informs the family of the strangled woman that the inheritance about which they were so concerned in the second act is not that of Mlle Lorpailleur at all but that of an uncle who died at the same time as her. Mlle Lorpailleur's inheritance is very small. All she inherited from her mother was a small house in the Rue des Casse-Tonnelles, which was rented out to second-hand dealers. The whole of the uncle's inheritance, which would have accrued to her had she lived, goes to the Waifs and Strays.

26

Adieu

Sophie Narre was the laundress at the Migeotte Laundry in Fontoine. She was red-haired and purple-nosed. And Soulevert was the grocer, and Ducreux the baker and all, I have bid them all adieu. "Adieu? Why adieu?" they asked. "It's just one of your expressions," I said.

Adieu Sinture, adieu all of you, your names stick in my throat. If I meet you again, I shall say hello, but if you think I'm going to concern myself with your activities, you've got something coming to you. You'll have to stand on your own feet from now on. Adieu!

PART II

MAHU TRIES TO TALK

I

The Door-Bell

What happens, for example, if you open the door to people who ring and they start talking about revelations? They certainly want to. They pretend they might have made a mistake. "You are So-and-so?" they ask. And if you say yes? They know you aren't. They come in. They start saying, "We Christians" or "We travellers". You're suspicious, you know when they say "we something" they don't in fact belong to that something. They just want to bother you. They pretend to belong to whatever they say they belong to, but they don't. They just want to worm secrets out of you, they want you to get involved and instead of helping you they start talking about revelations. Not about *us*, of course, but about themselves.

Why do they pretend to be *we something*? Why?

And then if you listen to their revelations, you're done for. It always begins with the truth. It's their little obsession. They tell you that they were overwhelmed by the truth, that they were looking for God and they found your door. And you could kick yourself for saying, "Yes, that's right. This is the So-and-sos' house." Because they are compelled, so as not to look as if they're lying, to say "Monsieur So-and so". And the revelations they make are so obviously right that you forget for the moment that they're about them. You think they're about you.

They go away. If you remember that So-and-so lives on the floor below, you call down to them that they've made a mistake and when you've shut the door again you go grrrrr grrrrr into your handkerchief. But what if you don't remember?

You should never open the door to people who are going to say *we something*. You can tell them by the way they ring the door-bell.

2

Germs

When you have an idea, what do you do with it? With me it's an illness, an abscess, but it doesn't come up from inside, I catch it like a germ, I detest ideas. As if everyone had 'flu, and one had to catch it. I'm always having to do things. I don't understand freedom. For example, my brothers go skiing. I don't like skiing, or rather I wouldn't think of going skiing and suddenly I am doing it myself. I didn't used to have the same tastes as everyone else and now I'm ashamed of the fact. I feel so out of it all, I am predisposed to an attack of ideas, I'm in incubation. I can never enjoy my own health, I'm always having to catch other people's germs. Why is that? My health is others' sickness. I think my real health would be a slow, lingering death. I don't know why I try to run away from it. The funny thing is that in the end I'd rather be ill, it keeps you on your feet, it gets you around a bit.

My sister said to me: "I dreamt I was in a car with a young man and I was at the wheel, but I wasn't driving, it was the young man beside me who was driving, he was driving very well, I had nothing to do when suddenly we had an accident, we weren't in the car any more, we were walking and all the young man had in his hands was the gear-lever and some sort of burnt thing, I was very annoyed at having to say when we got back, 'That's all that's left of the car!"

I love people to tell me about their dreams. Some people don't like to, but it's very instructive and amusing to make things up, or rather they've already been made up. You just have to let yourself go. Like my cousin who dreamt that I had painted an avenue of palm-trees at Cannes and everyone was walking up and down it saying, "This is the avenue that Mahu painted." I thought it was very nice of my cousin to dream that, but what does it mean? That I should go to Cannes and paint an avenue of palm-trees? And what about my sister's dream? That she'll marry an incendiary, or that she must take out a fire-insurance policy? When you dream about fire, it often means death, says Mlle Germaine, but there's no such thing as a dead car. The strangest thing is that you should be in someone else's dreams at all. I'm sure that if we slept all the time without eating, we'd live everywhere at once, but food makes us heavy and we stay where we are instead of flying about over different countries and different people having nightmares. We ought to be able to interrupt their dreams saying, for example to my cousin about the avenue of palm-trees, "Can't you see, it's much too difficult. I'd never paint that."

Do you think we are responsible for others' legs? Let's say, for example, that I'm going skiing and I forget to go and see Latirail who is to have his leg amputated. If I don't go and see him after his operation, but go instead to a football match or go skiing again, will they cut off his other leg as well? And if instead of getting my god-children their Christmas presents, I go and buy myself some cigarettes, will they go and break their legs?

How beautiful my part of the world is with its pear-trees and its valleys, Saint-Jean-de-Sixt, Saint-Jean-d'Aulph, Saint-Jeoire-en-Faucigny. I go skiing with my brothers, unless one of us has dislocated a knee cap or bashed his face in, and we call at inns and drink fresh milk and eat sauerkraut which gives me diarrhoea, and because of my tooth-ache I have to send a telegram to Latirail saying that I can't go and see him.

On the mountain road we passed a funeral procession, mind we don't crash the car into the hearse, that would be amusing, I was full up with Christmas biscuits and Italian panettone, a sort of sweet soufflé, a piece has to be kept in a cupboard and not be eaten until the feast of Saint-Blaise, it will stop you having sore throats. Another frontier custom! My brothers and I are frontiersmen through and through and that's my trouble, you see, I can never feel quite at home. But I love my frontier, my Savoy stretching as far as Cluses with its sorbs—what a magnificent name—and its pump-sheds.

3

The Curtain Chicken

"Oh, yes, we showed 'em how to ride a bike," she says, and she tastes her sauce, empties a glass at the bar, tastes her sauce again, wipes her hands on her apron and kisses a lady-customer who has just come in. It's not much of a place, but the hostess certainly has got something, with her belly and her hair always as it should be with its stove near the door, her son is a cyclist, she's mad about her cyclist, you can tell that, and she knows it, she says as much and I'm not saying anything that anyone doesn't know already, it's public knowledge. "Oh, yes, Madame, we showed 'em how to ride a bike, here's his photo, he won the race." Between a steak and a salad she quickly takes the photograph down from the wall, that's him, he won the race, a good-looker, eh?

It's as if she was the cyclist, she won the races, she says "we showed 'em," the *we* of love. What more can one say?

What funny letters I write! But what can I do, my breathing isn't good, there's my accent, my voice, I was born with them, so what can I do about it? If there aren't enough commas, or too many, blame my childhood. These childhood memories, they will keep coming back, it's really most annoying, it's as bad as Proust.

I was reminded of this when a friend of mine came to see me a moment ago and proudly announced, "We've got our curtains up now?" So naturally, of course, I'm a child again making a telephone call with the curtain-cords in my bedroom, there's a metal knob at the end, and I'm four years old, I telephone, "Hello, Granny, I've got a chicken here." It's the same thing. "I've got curtains." Don't you think so? There he is all proud, he's a grown-up isn't he, like me, and just look what he says and thinks. Talk about adults!

Rather than get no letters at all, I suppose you prefer to put up with the style and tap your feet when really I go too far. That's it, isn't it, you tap your feet.

When we were little, we used to say, "Bourdodzoï," which means in God's name, and "Chinicododzoï," for God's sake.

4

Almost

When you say "dragged out by the hair" it doesn't mean that what you say is dragged out by its own hair which, of course, it hasn't got, but quite simply that before saying it you really had to scratch your head and, instead of the idea emerging at once, you had to draw it out from the roots of the hair to the ends. It's a very delicate operation. Ideas obtained in this way are never very successful because they think fit, once they are out, to assume the average dimensions of the things one usually says, they seem to be in disguise. Generally speaking, people don't like disguise—which is why it is blamed for whatever one doesn't happen to like.

When you say "almost" it doesn't mean "at such and such a distance from something precise," but the exact opposite, that is to say: "The precise thing would be quite vague without the better, sharper thing beside it." You don't compare the thing before with the thing after, you say: "This thing after is so vague, it's a good job we have this thing before which shows it up better." "This fellow is almost an idiot" means that you know the fellow so well, you know so well what he is thinking, that when someone says "idiot" you know what it means because of him. "This speech is almost gibberish," you'd be hard put to think of gibberish by itself, it's the speech that has given you an idea of what it is. "This chocolate is almost the same as the chocolate I ate just now," you have already forgotten what the first one tasted like, it comes after, this second one reminds you, it comes before.

What is precise always precedes.

How easily we would understand one another if everyone took heed of simple things like that.

When you look through binoculars, you are holding an instrument of precision and you see very clearly a small cabin which would seem quite indistinct without the binoculars. So you say, "Well, well, it's just like another one I know, they are almost alike," and as soon as you say that you no longer see it, in your mind you are comparing it with the one you think came *before*, while, in fact, it comes after.

Truth means binoculars, precision, the thing that really comes first is the binoculars. You should say: "Well, well, these binoculars are almost the cabin." But you're not logical, you forget the binoculars and the thing you see comes first and the imaginary cabin second. You think you are progressing to an ever greater precision whereas in fact you are regressing, the only precision is what you have in your hands. Because of comparisons, we're always getting this crazy future—a false future, since by inventing the terms, you sink deeper and deeper into the past.

The best thing would be to stop comparing altogether. You'd then be sure that you liked something in the proper way. But perhaps that isn't possible. That's the way things are.

That's why I speak of things "dragged out by the hair." They have to be admitted.

5

Shortened Time

"Listen, you're always telling me I'm mad. Well, listen to what happened just now. I promise I won't change a word. I was on my way home. It was 11.30 p.m. And old woman stopped me in the street. She spoke with a Polish accent. She asked me for a light, which I gave her, and said: 'Do you live around here?' I said yes. 'Do you speak English?' I said no. 'Could you see me home? I've just been to the cinema and I haven't a sou on me. I need some matches. You couldn't give me some matches, could you?' I gave her my matches and do you know what she said? She said 'Thank you, Monsieur, thank you for England.' That's all. When I got home I boiled myself a cup of milk. A good cup of milk makes me feel much better at night. I then stuck some photographs in my scrap-book. That took about two hours. It was one o'clock by the time I'd finished."

"Well?"

"Then I had to go back to the *café-tabac*."

"Why?"

"Because I'd given my matches to the old woman . . . So I went back . . . You see, I wanted to tell you all this while it was still fresh in my mind, so that you can see what a life I lead. I said it all happened just now. But as I'm telling you about it, it gets further and further away. Before long, it'll be yesterday or the day before. The more I tell you exactly what happened, the further away it will get. If I told you everything, without missing anything out, it would have happened last year. I'll have to keep changing the date as I go along or you won't believe anything I tell you."

"I don't see what you mean."

"Well, since the incident of the old woman and the matches I've had time to drink my milk, stick in my photographs and go out to the *café-tabac*. I told you it took me nearly two hours to stick in my photographs. So that makes more than two hours, including the milk. It was not one o'clock when I went out, therefore, but one-thirty. At two o'clock I'm still in the café talking. So I shortened it by half-an-hour so that the beginning wouldn't get too far away. I gained half-an-hour by shortening it, so that it could stay just now and because I knew that if I didn't shorten it you wouldn't still be there. If I told you that the café was shut and that it took me till four o'clock to find one that was open and that I then went to bed, it would be yesterday already. Do you see? A whole day wasted. And if I went on in this way, telling you everything, you wouldn't still be there to listen to me. Or you'd be there in three weeks, four weeks, eight months, a year. And I'd never have had time to tell you everything I've just told you. It would take another year before I got round to saying, 'Just now an old woman stopped me in the street,' and it would all start all over again, it would take years to tell you everything, I'd lose half-an-hour, then another half-hour, then another, I'd shorten weeks, months, years, what I'd gain in half-hours I'd lose in truth. Do you see? If I said 'just now' it would be no longer true, because years would have intervened, and yet it was just now. I have to say so. It's the truth. Do you see now why one can't recount anything? You see it's not because I'm mad."

6

Six o'clock

Supposing you wake up at six o'clock on a winter's morning, and it's a week-day, a day-off, say, or an ordinary day for those who start work later, and instead of going back to sleep, you get up. If you're not alone and your wife wakes up, she asks, "What are you doing?" and you reply, "I'm going to take the dust-bin downstairs. I forgot it last night." She agrees and goes back to sleep.

You put some light clothes on, so as to feel the cold, an anorak for example, and you set out, with your hands in your pockets and your shoulders hunched up to your ears, for the Halles. At this time in winter, the Rue de Rivoli is still full of lorries and behind the street the markets are in full swing.

You find it difficult to see anything. You have to relax and lower your shoulders. You often go to the Halles. You're no stranger to the markets. This time it's tripe you're there for.

MENU

Tongues, with lower tongue and stumps and a huge white thing, which is the gullet, in any case the tongue itself is less than half of the whole piece.

Liver.
Lungs.
Fats.
Hearts.
Ears.
Tails.
Marrow bones.
Sweetbreads, perhaps.
Raw ox-heads without hairs.

Raw ox-heads with hairs.

Calf-heads, cooked, raw, halves, on trolleys, on counters, on tables, on lino.

Feet.

Groins.

Then there's always a nun standing next to half a sheep's carcase, waiting for it to be cut up.

White overalls, berets, rubber boots, leather jackets, shawls.

Porters, signed on for a few hours' work, load and unload the lorries.

Fires in braziers.

Counters, adders, weighers, loaders, intermediaries.

"What can I do for you, Monsieur?'

"Nothing. I'm just looking."

You go and have a coffee. You could get through a dozen croissants. Bernard says to Robert, "Bordeaux beat Saint-Etienne 2—1."

That's today, just once. At other times, you only go for the flowers or to smell the tangerines and the leaks. In summer there are men selling ferns.

But I'm not much good at talking. You don't get up at six in the morning to talk, but to see. I'd rather see than talk any day.

You don't know what you take back to your wife? A nice little notice "PLEASE CHECK YOUR CHANGE AT THE CASH-DESK." You can either pinch them from the stalls or buy them in the Rue des Prouvaires in front of the Café de la Tête Noire.

7

Butter

"The hardest thing of all, don't you think, is not being able to say the word that's coming."

"What word?"

"Well, 'butter', for example. Suppose I'm talking to you. I talk, talk, talk. Sentences, nothing but sentences. At a certain moment, I'm about to say 'butter'. I suddenly feel it. I was going to say it. I quickly say something else, fortunately. Because when you feel you're going to say something, a word, 'butter' for example, even if you realise it just before saying it, your head was full of it beforehand willy-nilly. Your head was full of butter. You had to talk, talk, talk so that suddenly you could say 'butter'. But if you say it, hey presto, your head's empty again, and you don't know what to say next. It's terrible when, what's more, you realise that the person you're talking to already knows that you're going to say 'butter' or she is also thinking about it. Because then her head is also emptied the moment you say 'butter' and you both stand there not knowing what to say next. That's much worse. Because, what's more, when you know beforehand what you're going to say, the other person, even if she doesn't know yet, or doesn't suspect anything or doesn't think about it willy-nilly, she isn't listening. If you want to prove to her that you like butter, and, moreover, your head is completely empty since you thought of it beforehand and you don't know what to say next, but let's suppose that you know by heart what you're going to say and that's not real words, is it, well, the other person won't be listening. If you think a word beforehand, not only does it empty your head, it cuts off its own head, it obliterates its own meaning. For 'butter', for example, there is no more butter. Anywhere. You've never eaten butter. You don't know there is such a thing. If I think about my future, I haven't got any future. You know, sometimes, I'm afraid of having revelations. Just now I walked past a building with a large clock. And I said to myself, supposing that clock were to make revelations to me? Supposing I were to know what was to become of me? It would strike me dead on the spot. Because when you know beforehand what you're going to be you become empty. Then it's not a matter of your head, or of a word you think, it's you. I'm afraid. When I think about it, I have to say grrrrr grrrrr into my hand or into my handkerchief so as to get it out of my head. Then it stops. You're all right on the edge of the pavement. I always walk on the very edge. No one can get in your way there. You're free."

8

Movements

When you walk, do you think what you're doing? No, of course you don't. Neither do I, usually. But sometimes I hear my feet. It's most annoying. You don't, do you? I hear them and I can't block my ears up. So, guess what I do? I walk like the other people I meet. I look at them quickly before they pass behind me, or if they pass in front of me, I follow them. It's the easiest thing in the world really. In this way, you change step about twelve times every hundred metres and you find yourself at the theatre. The shops are made of cardboard. You can move them about as you like. You ask as you tell them and you buy them a drink. They always drink when eating. Goats' cheese. Do you like goats' cheese? I don't. Anyway, if the shops are bistros you're playing on velvet. You've got some reason to buy people drinks. When you're by yourself don't you ever want to buy people drinks? Or buy all the cigarettes they've got behind the bar and hand them out? I do. Then everyone shakes hands with you. They drink to your health. The landlord has a twin brother. It's true, I'm not pulling your leg. Who's so much like him that you can play a trick on the chap you're talking to. The other day, it was young Pinson. I said, "Look outside." He looked outside. And then I said, "Now look at the landlord." He looked at the landlord. I said, "Well, it's someone else." But it was the same one. The twin brother wasn't there. Pinson had never seen them together. I played the trick in order to make him realise that they looked alike. A funny way of going about it, eh? Pinson said I was cracked.

There were also some Italians who complained of the cold. They were near the door. They changed places in order to get out of the draught. And then they moved again. The operators were laughing at them. A tall woman came in who looked at you on all sides at once. It was a bit embarrassing. You wondered how long she'd be before she was satisfied. It was the sequences. One sequence cut your hand as you held your glass, another ran up your arm as you were looking for your handkerchief and another spoke to you in English because of the director. "I am an exile," said the women. They sounded so sad that you asked them to have a drink as well. They're rather like Picassos with all those eyes and their noses inside out. There was a reproduction in the window of a Picasso painting and underneath was written: "Don't look like that. Leave your pen with us for 24 hours. All repairs. Modest prices."

It's a terrifying experience talking to the cinema. Do you know, she knows everything. She talks in the infinitive and future perfect. Directors, producers, even the electricians. There were two of them in the room. The cinema didn't even look at them. Well, anyway, with these women going on in their sad Russian voices about being exiles, we began to wonder what we were doing there. Some thought of committing suicide. But all that does is fill up the headlines. This war, is it a war of ideas? I touch it with my finger. I'm afraid to pick up my glass. You think I'm drunk, don't you? Touch it, then. Touch my glass. It'll explode. It's electric.

Is it true that the mind swallows whatever it touches? But my finger isn't my mind. You think it's my finger that's fighting the war? I can't touch anything? Answer, answer me!

No, you prefer my ideas, don't you? It would hurt too much to answer. It would cut the current. You're scared.

An old man once predicted that I would succeed. What did he mean? That I would succeed at what? Not carrying parcels, I suppose . . . Should I change my job? I bet you're going to tell me to find a good office. It's no good. First, I can't type, secondly, I can't bear offices. Even the idea of going in to one . . .

This old fellow said to me: "When you speak the words flow through your hands, your neck, your spinal column.

While you've been talking I've been watching you. I am deaf, but I understood everything you said. You speak in images, through your movements. It reminds me of my youth. We used to talk like that. You will see, when you're old you can't move and you become deaf."

9

Rest

Just for a rest. It's even better than sleep. And not as dangerous. Sleep might go on for several days, don't you think? And how hard it is to get used to things again afterwards! So, just like this, you see. You lie down on your bed, or on the floor, you press your hands to your ears and you turn over with your backside in the air and your feet over your head. I can rest like that. Either that, or combing my hair for a long time with something hard. Dog brushes are best. If you haven't got any, you can use anything pointed. And it cures you of visits. They just go out of your head. I have so many sometimes. The most annoying are the ones that don't come. They have friends and acquaintances who ask your advice. You say you don't know anything about the matter, but you already know you'll have to say something. Oh, yes . . .

So, in the midst of it all, you get what rest you can.

Or you can rest by dancing. You dance as you like. But you must make a lot of turns. You then lose your balance and your tiredness. Or if you shout out whatever comes into your head, that can do you a lot of good too. Isn't it Indians who do that? Or Africans? I can see why.

10

Balance

I was at the back of the hall, by the pillars, but I wasn't in the right mood to listen to the speaker. You're not always in the right mood. So I looked at the people standing in front of me or beside me. Well, have you ever thought that when a chap is standing he's in perfect balance? I hadn't. You only have to look at him. You concentrate, for example, on his ear and at the same time on some unmoving point. I used the side of a pillar. And you see that the ear never stops moving for a moment. It swings from left to right, up and down. The whole head and the whole body swings, right down to the feet. It's the feet that keep the balance constant. With practice, you see that you don't need to look at anything else at the same time. You can see that the ear is constantly moving and that all these chaps are moving, from side to side, backwards and forwards. You begin to feel dizzy.

I said to myself: supposing they realised they were balancing, supposing they constantly felt the effort exerted by their feet, their legs, their backs, their necks? I've an idea they wouldn't be able to remain for long. It would be too tiring. It wouldn't be very convenient for public meetings. There'd be nobody to listen. The speakers would blame it all on to obligatory balance. Because it always boils down to the same thing: as soon as we know we have to do something, we give it up. I'm like that. I think that's why one never talks to someone about his balance. Note that it would be exactly the same sitting on a chair. It's a little less effort, but the ears certainly move around.

II

The Newspaper

This is what I read this morning in a real newspaper, belonging to Mlle Germaine:

THE ABBEY CHURCH OF THE ABBEY OF NOTRE-DAME DE SAILIS.

His Excellency Mgr Lahieu, Bishop of Arc and Dux, has consecrated the abbey church of Notre-Dame de Sailis.

The Sanctuary of Sailis, situated in the heart of Tralosse, on a gently sloping hill, is claimed to be a thousand years old.

Recently handed over to the Benedictines of Mont-Jolivet and established as an abbey church, the new church was built almost eighty years ago. But it was still awaiting its solemn consecration.

The ceremony was performed by Mgr Lahieu in the presence of Their Excellencies Mgr Verrier, Bishop of Batonne; Mgr Saint-Jacques, Bishop of Lordus; the Very Rev Abbots of Sailis, of Rec, of Gelloc and of Lamiran; the Very Rev Coadjutor of Gelloc; and Monsignori Donaste, Chadiro, Micarry and Saint-Firmin.

A truly splendid ceremony in which, apart from the Benedictine monks, about a hundred priests and a great many friends and other faithful participated. It ended with the singing of Pontifical High Mass, celebrated by the Very Rev Abbot of Sailis.

During Pontifical Vespers, sung by the Abbot of Lamiran, a sermon given by the Bishop of Batonne provided a fitting tribute to the ancient church.

His Excellency Mgr Saint-Jacques celebrated Benediction, and so the ceremonies that had begun in the light mist of an ideal autumn morning, and continued during a day of warm, yet gentle sunlight, ended just at the dawn of a new day.

Underneath there is a large photograph the whole width of the page, full of soutanes, robes, surplices, copes, stoles, mitres, crosses, joined hands, Gothic arches, foliage, a procession of people dressed in white against a black background that looks rather like a spindle hedge; on the left of the picture is the branch of a cedar-tree.

Further on in the paper, I found this:

AT GASSEIILE, SPLENDID CELEBRATIONS OF THE FEAST OF ST SEBASTIENNE DE VALERE. This saint, canonised by Pius XV, lived for many years in Gasseille. Received, a hundred years ago, by Mgr de Hazedot, she found there a refuge from persecution. She died in Gasseille in 1586, after a lifetime of fruitful labours. The mother-house of the Sisters of St Léon de l'Apparition today enjoys a period of great prosperity.

The festivities began on Friday 17 October, in the presence of His Excellency Mgr Noussahon, Archbishop of Aty, who thus linked his diocese, in which Sébastienne de Valère was born, with that of Gasseille.

In his panegyric of the saint, the Rev Father Ayaud, SJ, showed how sanctity could . . .

The newspaper was torn at this point. The paper had been used where it should not have been used. I began again at the next column:

mic of St Sébastienne by emphasising the virtues of the nun, and His Excellency Mgr de Pervenchènes, Archbishop of Arc, gave the Blessing of the Most Holy Sacrament.

On Sunday, Mgr Lesga, counsellor of the nunciature of Chavis, celebrated a communion mass in the chapel of the mother-house. Later, at the cathedral, Pontifical High Mass was sung by His Excellency Doncaille, the Apostolic Nuncio. A particularly dense crowd filled the vast church. A dense but also a very quiet crowd that participated devoutly in the liturgical ceremonies. The same day, in the church of St Léon, the church of great solemnities a . . .

It was torn again.

As I copied out the article, I wondered if it was all true.

But it must be, it was written down. Every day, journalists write these accounts. Every day, Mlle Germaine reads them in her paper. How happy you must be, Mlle Germaine!

12

Mademoiselle Germaine

I am very nervous. I was in the W.C. I could hear a wireless on the floor above. A singer was singing: "And the duck crouched down, ha-ha-ha . . ." I was very annoyed. I pulled the chain immediately. It didn't work. I shut the door. As I was going out I passed someone who said: "My name's Germaine, you know, I'm forty years old, I've been working for twenty years, I made a mistake, if I'd listened to Odette I wouldn't be here now, she has four children, a maid and a car, they go to the country every Sunday, Ernest is never unfaithful to her, but everyone isn't Ernest. My nephew's a washer-up on board a steamer, at the moment, that is, he's always changing his job, he causes me a lot of worry. I've just bought a sewing-machine and he asks me for money. If I hadn't bought the sewing-machine . . . What does he want to do with the money? Women again, I suppose. Well, this time the answer's no. I want to do something with my own life. These girls who go with any man they see, pooh, my Dad used to say: 'My girl, while ever you're under this roof you're my daughter.' And, anyway, it doesn't bother me, after all, why should I care, there are girls who are more unhappy than me, eh?"

I say to her: "Mademoiselle, your father was right. I know your nephew. He's a fine lad, you know! Sell your sewing-machine, that will get him out of trouble."

It worked. She seemed flattered. I went home, that is I got as far as my door. Supposing that story of the crouching duck was true? Supposing I was to find him doing goodness knows what? Supposing he were to write that one hadn't the right to be a crouching duck, that he was the only one who . . . etc . . .? Perhaps I'd better hang around a bit. So I went back into the street. And I went to Latirail's. Ninette answered the door and began behaving in a very strange way. She said that artists' wives were always unhappy, that she was very intelligent, that I should say so to her husband, and, still crying, she went out to do the shopping. I found Latirail making faces in the mirror.

13

Letter—Obstacle

I got a letter. I read it, unfortunately, and put it on the mantelpiece. I should have burnt it, but even now I can't. It was written by a woman. A jealous woman. Her letter questions the influence of Mlle Germaine. It throws doubt on my sincerity. I can't have that. It's not my fault if, in general, I know a great many people and, in particular, Mlle Germaine. You take where you find. You aren't more sincere if you avoid dangerous company than if you frequent it. Nor more intelligent if you pass judgement on them. I met Mlle Germaine one day because our paths happened to cross. In order not to have been there, it would be necessary not to have lived at all. If Latirail makes faces it's because he isn't always Latirail. And if, in order to hear a noise, you have to cut out all other noises, then you have a right to do so. When you explain to friends what you are doing and why, you tell them everything without asking yourself if it's logical. You don't listen to yourself. You get rid of one explanation—and one's as good as another. Friends who throw things back in your face are treacherous.

This woman in the letter is treacherous. I ought to burn it. But I'm afraid that later I'll begin to think I never said anything to her. It would be just the same if I tore it up. She's now throwing back in my face what I was at that moment. If I tore it up, I should tear myself up. No. I must leave it on the mantelpiece. You need yourself. It's enough to make you feel sick.

I saw some people on the sixth floor who had visitors. The visitors were on the ground floor. The people on the sixth floor, who were very intelligent, wanted to tell their visitors how to work the lift. Why, then, did they whisper, instead of shouting? The visitors on the ground floor couldn't hear what they were whispering. The people on the sixth floor began to get impatient and call them names. They had every right to, because I learnt that they had suffered a great deal to become intelligent. But what about their visitors? I also learnt that even if they'd heard what the people on the sixth floor were whispering they wouldn't have been able to use it. They were one-armed. Nor could they ignore the lift and go up the stairs—they were legless. So they settled down like campers on the ground floor, in the entrance hall. We were always getting in their way. There were so many of them that the police were powerless to do anything. The building would have to be burnt down. You always hesitate before burning anything. Like my letter. Latirail burnt his, but they weren't abusive. Fire is a temptation. You think about it. And sometimes you give in to it.

But supposing this woman who wrote to me happened to be on the ground floor? Supposing her treachery had made her one-armed? I should find myself with the people on the sixth floor . . . whispering the secret of how the lift works. No, I don't want that. I'm not intelligent. I don't want to suffer. I must go downstairs at once. I must take the letter off the mantelpiece and forgive her.

Where is she? Did Sinture give her to me? Perhaps I just supposed . . . And yet it's all because of her, this business of the visitors . . . Unless Sinture told me about them?

A bad day. The one-armed visitors invade the hall. When you see them close to, they're not one-armed at all. They're sheep.

14

The Tsarina

What's that beggar-woman called now? The princess, or countess, or queen, or tsarina, with a scarf under her bonnet, she sleeps on the Pont-Neuf, I think she's Polish or Czecho-Slovak, do you know the one I mean? She's no ordinary beggar, she's my mother by marriage. It was she who said, "Thank you, my child," when I gave her my *céleri rémoulade*. I had nothing left to eat and I'm sure the tasarina made up the "my child," but what is said is said, I must call her mother next time.

So I went back to the shop and bought some more celery. There were a hundred grammes, which meant sixty francs on the scales. I'm sure they make it up, they say sixty and you pay and that's that, the same as with mother-tasarina. Incidentally, a barman once said to an old lady, "Warm enough Mother?" She didn't look at all pleased. Do you know what she said? She said, "Don't call me Mother, I don't like the term." It's true! Not that I don't like making things up, but sometimes it's really not worth it. "I don't like the term!" The old bag! But perhaps she couldn't help it after all. Yet I looked at her, I looked closely to see her eyes, but she was staring into her cup.

Do you like people? I think I must be abnormal. It seems it can be unhealthy to like anyone at all like that. Have you any illusions? Illusions are when to go into a baker's shop to buy a lemon. Funny, isn't it?

15

Pronunciation

These faces you see talking, these people with faces talking, one here, the other opposite, they look such block-heads sometimes I wonder how they understand each other, nothing moves on them, there's a nose, little eyes and cheeks that are of the same skin as the forehead and nostrils, you'd think they were machines that were talking for the first time. I listen, I listen and the fact is they don't understand each other, one asks for some sugar and the other one gives him a sandwich. Or they're in a café, one of them is talking about something and the other one answers, but they don't always understand each other, they use words but they might as well not bother for all the good it is. They might just as well scratch themselves or look for fleas. Why?

Are people talking to themselves when they move their lips as they're walking or are they just pretending to so that you'll try and hear what they're saying? Supposing it was you they were muttering to themselves? Supposing they were saying, "Mahu, Mahu . . ." But, of course, you'd see that they weren't the right syllables. But supposing they were telegrams?

When you're expecting bad news you have to be prepared for it a long time ahead so that when the telegram comes you can already pronounce the syllables in your mouth before opening it.

Children amuse me. Have you noticed how they speak inside out? Or rather they sing or form sounds, a sound, like that, while they're playing, a sound or a song or a cry inside out, drawing instead of pushing. It's too difficult to explain.

16

And then

And then there are those musicians who haven't got pianos, they seem to manage all the same. You see them sitting in cafés with a score open in front of them, or they write music. Anyway I saw a Chinaman doing that. Or if they have got pianos, perhaps they rehearse before their concert; they live too far away, they haven't the time, unless they quickly write down what sounds they can pick up around them, it's rather special. I can understand in a way. But aren't they making a mistake? I'm thinking of the Chinaman. A glass put down on the bar is D, all right. The door of the telephone-cabin is sharp. The noise of people talking, the métro underneath and the neon-lights are the percussion, all right. But wouldn't he hear better in his own room?

Obviously, someone doing a crossword is very pleased when someone else sitting at the same table says the word for 6 down that begins with *ZA*, it's what's known as co-operation. And: "Her curiosity proved stronger than her obedience," three letters beginning with *EV*. He couldn't find the word. "It's mythology," he said. "No," I said, "it's the Bible, it's EVE." All right, I was very pleased at finding it because a chap who does crosswords is always a bit of a nuisance, especially if he says, "I was doing them before you were born."

When someone says, "Oh, you're lucky, I've always wanted to do what you do," if you do painting for example it's annoying to have to listen to that sort of thing, because it's not luck at all, it's more like an infirmity.

17

The Stone

Without intending to, I kicked a stone along the pavement which was covered with litter, and the stone hit the foot of a lady who was coming towards me. She cried, "Oo", and I laughed. I said, "I'm sorry, it's nothing to do with me," but I don't think she heard me, she was furious. I find that very amusing. Supposing you threw a stone at one of those big Cadillacs as you went by and they started swearing at you in a deep, American drawl.

I know an old lady who says: "When an American treads on your foot he is 'sorry' and you are chocolate." The same lady went into a shop to buy some lavatory paper. "Would you like it scented?" the assistant asked. "No, washable please," she replied.

I know so many funny stories and yet I'm not laughing all the time. It's a pity. And a great many horrible stories, too. This one, for example, about another woman I knew, who died from poisoning, locked up by her husband, a frightful little husband with a crooked head, it leans to the side, it's muscular, I think, he holds it straight with his walking-stick when he's in company. Well, he was a drug addict, he had an old mistress and made his wife live with her and gradually he drugged his wife, a bit more each time, she never left her room, she cried when people went to see her, it seems, no one knew exactly what was happening, she was more and more in love with her husband, with his strong will, very gradually she died, and the other woman pretended to look after her.

A friend of ours who has two children told me how one day the little boy said to his sister, "Do you know what suppositories are? They're sweets for your bottom."

18

The Specialists

Fishermen in the Luxembourg Gardens are fishing for gold fish with rubber boots and shrimp-nets. It's so cold! They can't put their hands in their pockets, and, God knows, I should think their feet are having a time. One of the men says, "They're all there now" and in fact all the remaining fish are there, the others are belly-up in the mud. They're draining the big lake. While quite a way off I saw something in it. I said, "It's ice, it's so cold" but it's mud, close up. One of the men has found a boat in the middle of the lake and is arranging it under the Cupids of the fountain. "A young carp," says the first fisherman, and he throws it into one of the buckets with the other fish. The buckets are then put on to an electric trolley and emptied into the Médicis fountain.

God, it's cold! But I have to admit that I'm enjoying myself. It's a real sight this draining operation and then there are the onlookers making remarks. There are two next to me who talk foreign. It's as if they make up silly words on purpose, they must be Orientals. Really, I'm sure they make up the words. I'd like to ask them, "What language are you speaking?" and add, "It's very beautiful," but I daren't. They move away and I walk over to the Médicis fountain. There is a distinguished-looking old gentleman in an Astrakhan coat who must be bored to death. He stops. One of the workers who is looking at the fish bursts out laughing, and says, "It's dead," and he's right, one of the fish, several of them in fact, are dead, they're floating on the water, and I thought to myself, "They couldn't stand the change." And I say to myself that I could be one of those fellows, they're probably men who were looking for a job, unless they're specialists. There're so many specialists in Paris, I've only go to ask them, why not. It really is worth the trouble to learn a job when one could be a goldfish emptier, or let's call it a lake drainer so as not to get confused with those who clean the fish, like the women at Bastia who can take out the liver or the roe in one go, they're really specialists. Bastia is an old port, really old, it's a pity it's not very well known, it isn't on the continent.

You learn a job and you then have to read the papers in order to keep up to date. It's a hard job keeping up to date when there are lake drainers.

There is Sainte Mathilde, a queen of the Luxembourg Gardens who's having her foot changed in the middle of a lot of scaffolding. You can see her from below, with her stone plaits, surrounded by her planks and the dark branches of the chestnut-trees. From her lofty vantage she looks straight out in the direction of the fish. In the scaffolding is an Algerian knocking in nails and a Norman wearing clogs is talking to him, they're sure to be specialists, they're foot-changers. But suddenly this queen, rising up between an Algerian and a Norman, takes on a magical quality.

I find it difficult to make myself clear. It's getting worse. This business of talking, that's what the trouble's all about.

19

Curare

When I got to Latirail's for dinner Ninette was in the kitchen, she said, "They're already there," they being the other guests, a husband and his wife. I stayed with Ninette and opened the oysters, I'd brought seven smallish oysters, just to taste. Ninette was delighted, I opened the oysters with her scissors, be careful of my nice new scissors, and I rinsed the opened oysters under the tap, pity there isn't any sea water, tap water will take the taste away. And I also had six large snails to show Ninette how to cook them. When everything was ready Ninette opened the door and said, "We're eating these little things first." No, I forgot before cooking the snails that I was going to see Latirail and the guests. They were talking about the clap, it seems it's much more annoying than a cold, I've never had it, and syphilitics. Latirail said that Indians were syphilitic, or was it Red Indians, anyway we talked about Indians and Latirail had been sawing shelves for the cupboard and the husband said that a piece of wood that was left over looked like a boomerang. That's it, it was then that we started talking about Indians. It seems that boomerangs come back to where they start from and the Indians have got a poison called curare that paralyses the muscles, and other poisons used in compresses for prisoners' joints, and blow-pipes. The Aztecs and Incas are very advanced civilisations and their architecture is as magnificent as that of the Egyptians. They're very interesting, these conversations at Latirail's, very intellectual. The lady-guest is a psychiatrist, you never know whether she's talking or whether she's just pretending to so as to make you talk, she might be taking notes, so to speak, for her scientific work. It's crazy, all these stories about Indians and poisons. It was then that Ninette said to me, "We might do something about the snails." We'd already cooked them and eaten them with the oysters before sitting down for dinner. Ninette had made a *quiche lorraine*. "It's superfine," said the psychologist looking at me.

After dinner we changed places. I was wearing a big hat pulled down over my eyes, or rather a cap made of wool and something that covers the ears, neck and chin, what's it called? A balaclava, I think. They lend it me when it's cold, I was lying across the sofa so that my head leaned forwards a bit because of the slope, I was very comfortable like that, the lamp cast a white light over everything. The others were sitting on the sofa or on the floor and we had to tell funny stories. My head was getting very hot, that visor thing was coming down over my eyes. I told them the story of the flies when we were at school. We used to catch big fat flies and stick coloured papers on their wings, red, blue, green, all kinds of colours, and the flies couldn't fly any more, they dragged themselves along the ground, they made little jumps, it was like moving papers. We used to put them on the ground in front of the old man's chair and when he saw these papers moving about, he thought he was having visions because of his stomach aches, he turned his head away but the flies were still there when he looked again. It was very useful, we could recite anything at all so long as it was the right length, he just wasn't listening, he was only thinking about the flies.

We talked about that and I felt very happy, I couldn't see anything, the visor was down, nothing but a bit of lamp and the husband's hair. They filled up my glass with brandy and I said that everyone was good. They said no, even children were cruel, there were people who killed or who robbed the blind, I said I was sure there weren't. People are wicked, the idea of revenge is responsibility, the lady psychiatrist agreed with me, she makes tests, she can see wickednesses in little squares and writing in flies' legs, flies with papers stuck to their wings that jump about, it made me want to laugh as if the lamp had a shirt on that it lifted and said, "Look at my flies."

This brandy isn't curare, what a delicious invention, a sweet poison that paralyses your limbs.

20

The House

I went with Latirail and Ninette to look around an old mill. It was a Saturday in winter. Latirail came to fetch me, he's done nothing, he can't work, he said. We walked around this cold, deserted mill that had just been bought by some rich people. They weren't there. The caretaker lived next door and his wife very kindly took us round. She said, "They want to come and spend the New Year here before the men start work on it, but you can see it's all falling to bits, they want to put a stove in his room just for the time being, but you can see this little stove is much too small, so I said to them, 'Why don't you have my cooker, I'm expecting a new one for my daughter's engagement. I'm hoping to have it in a few days.' They'd be much warmer then. She's my second daughter. The eldest got married at the beginning of the war, I don't want to do anything more for the younger one, imagine, she's only eighteen, she's in no hurry to get married. But her fiancé lives with us, it's better that way. It's dead round here. When I first came here a month ago that's what I thought, but the mistress said, 'You'll see in summer how wonderful it is here.' Meanwhile, my husband has found that the water seeps up through the floor, they'll have to dig it up and lay down new concrete, the repairs are nowhere near finished. Would you like some cider? I have some very good cider and my vinegar, do you like cider vinegar? It's the best vinegar, you know."

Ninette said she would have a litre of vinegar. We smelled it, it was very scented, with a sprig of rosemary in the bottle. While they drank the cider, I roamed around the mill, there were rotten staircases and beams. I was thinking about negroes, I'm always thinking about negroes and it could be that their magic is what we call depression or bad luck, but they dance and rid themselves of misfortune, while we get sad and visit tumble-down old mills.

It's funny how rich people have several houses, they make repairs in the depressions that other people have abandoned.

There was a red flower in a field, but when I got nearer I saw that it was a red cabbage all frizzy and gone to seed, I picked it to make a bouquet. The sky became red-cabbage pink, a tall walnut-tree hung over the mill and in the background were trees overgrown with mistletoe.

The caretaker's wife said that they were going to gather some mistletoe to decorate their banquet, she's given them the address for the goose, they'll roast it in the chimney oven, it's still waddling around. When she went out to get the vinegar, Ninette said, "Is she French, though? She makes grammar mistakes." Latirail replied, "How do you know that it isn't us who're making the mistakes?" I was looking at my red cabbage, and I haven't even got a vase, I'll have to give it to Ninette. I thought of the houses that engage servants, I can't live in my shed any more, I can only just recognise it, I sometimes make a mistake and sleep somewhere else. Supposing I had a talk with the caretaker's wife or with the new owner? I could have a contract to clear your trees of mistletoe, Madame, in exchange for a room.

I can't learn magic, what would I look like? It's not mine. I'm going to replace it now I've got a room, I'll invite all the negroes, we'll form a zone against depression and the rich won't need to buy ruins any more.

21

The Belly Dance

A moukere or a fatma or a mousmee was moving her belly, it was a belly dance. She's got rolls of fat and strings of pearls that hang down, and a specially big roll of fat just below her navel, I couldn't see very well, so I turned round a bit in my chair, she's got large soft breasts with a deep divide. The belly rotates and spirals upwards as far as the hips, Ninette was helping me to some *cous-cous* and Latirail was sitting right opposite the dancer. There are three rolls of fat, I think, one near the navel and the others going from the breasts to the arm-pits. She was twisting and turning metal castanets around her head, it was enough to burst your ear-drums. The mutton in the *cous-cous* was as tough as leather, but it's interesting how she moves her fat around even though it's so soft she does it so that people will put notes under her belt. Latirail gave her one, I asked him what it was like to feel. Ninette is eating, she says, "Excellent." I find it annoying having to do two things at once. I like *cous-cous*, but it would be better if she could do her dance afterwards, so that we could get on with eating and not have to keep looking at her belly. She kneels down and starts moving her titties, but her skirt gets on my nerves, it would be nicer to see everything, after all there are dancers who dance with nothing on, so I don't see why this one should be half-dressed. I ask Latirail if he thinks she has any hairs, she hasn't any under her arms, he says they're shaved. "Some more sauce?" Ninette asks, I say yes but I don't like the carrots and this sauce is full of carrots, you might just as well have a good *pot-au-feu* at home without all the pepper, especially as we're not drinking much, Latirail is at the end of the month.

She's off again, twisting and turning, If I could turn right round I might see better, but Ninette is eating and Latirail is doing both, they've got a good view, but I'm getting cricks in my neck and those castanets are giving me the staggers. Couldn't she just stop moving for a moment? If it's not that it's the paprika. Anyway this white roll of fat jerking its way upwards in front of her thighs, these clothes are really too tight. I can see the point of oases with fountains and cushions and baggy trousers. I wouldn't mind putting a note beside that belly and letting my hand slip down a bit, she's coming this way, she's coming over here, the mousmee's smiling at me. Better to say to yourself, "Put your hand down and leave it at that," I daren't ask Latiral for another note, perhaps one eats *cous-cous* at the same time to give one's hand something to do.

The proprietor asks me if it's good. I say yes and they're still singing the same song with banjos and castanets, even her backside moves. You could slip a note down that huge divide between her breasts, pity, other people are doing, we're broke of course. Ninette's eating her *cous-cous*, mine's cold. For a laugh, I asked Latirail whether he thought the rest moved underneath as well, and he said, "You don't change, do you? We take you out to an Algerian night-club and you can think of nothing but obscenities." I was quite taken aback, what does he think about, when he sees rolls of fat? His novel? He's got so much work it makes no difference whether he sees anything or not, he should have sat in my place with his back to the dancer, we didn't think about it.

If that's what oases are like, then I've no objections, but let's have it without *cous-cous*, or after *cous-cous*, unless we can go straight on to the harem. What's it like in a harem, anyway? What I'd like most would be the stuffed dates that make you fat, and the Turkish baths, all those fat women in the steam. But Ninette thinks I look too much instead of eating while it's hot.

22

Stilts

Supposing I wore stilts? It would change everything. When you went out for your coffee in the morning you'd put on your coat or something longer to hide your feet, and the pieces of wood would show underneath. The grocer's wife would say, "There goes spindleshanks for his morning drink, it must be nine o'clock." I'd cross the road without waiting for the green light, the cars would stop at the sight of a man on stilts and you might get your newspaper for nothing, at first anyway.

The technique of going down stairs would be a bit tricky, but I could walk down on foot and get up on to my stilts at the bottom step, or at the last but one which is about the right height.

I'd get them to serve my coffee on the shelf where the croissants are kept, or even higher with the old papers. They'd have to have some step-ladders that they'd use just for me and which would be kept between the telephone directories and the door marked PRIVATE. But they'd soon get used to it, François knows that at nine o'clock he'd get out the steps and put my coffee up on the shelf, and at five-past nine, "Good morning, Monsieur," "Good morning, François." He could even put my coffee up earlier if it suited him, I don't like it too hot.

To sit down, you just lean against the wall, with the stilts at a slight angle and lodged against the bar or a pillar. You can also crouch down. You might let people walk between your legs—it would be a help to the waiters—but if it's someone you can't abide, you could trip him up, a man on stilts could get away with it.

How delightful it would be! You'd no longer have to go through doors that were too low—it's what's known as natural selection. You can make your own stilts by buying planks of wood from the market near the Hôtel de Ville, you can get anything there. It's very tempting all that wood, it smells of vinegar a bit. I think I'll give my god-children wooden presents for Christmas, wooden books. You hesitate to give something you like as a present, in the end you don't know which you like best, the wood or the person, and you wish the person was made of wood so that you can like them both equally.

23

Conscientiousness

I took an anorak to Coutin that Leaumont had given me for Senet, he hadn't time to go himself. Coutin wasn't at home, his door was locked. I said to the concierge, "Would you give M. Coutin this anorak for Senet on behalf of Leaumont? My name's Mahu." I thought it was a bit complicated so I wrote him a note. "Coutin, underlined, from Leaumont for Senet, Mahu, underlined." The concierge needn't explain anything now.

But then I think: supposing I'd signed it with another name? That would have added a fifth person. Or two more names? From the point of view of the concierge, I'd have represented two more people, being the messenger of Leaumont, Senet and Coutin, and also of Coutin by himself since if he had been at home I'd have had nothing to say to the concierge. It's exactly the same as if I was Coutin asking me for Leaumont's anorak for Senet; or, to put it another way, if I, Mahu, sign myself Fernand or Karyer I'm making them think about the anorak, I'm making Coutin, it's just the same, think about Fernand and Karyer as well as the two others. I am making Karyer think about it *for me*, even if he knows nothing about it when Coutin telephones him and asks him what time he brought it. And as far as Leaumont is concerned, it was he, of course, who gave me the anorak, but what if I sign myself Fernand? And what if Fernand isn't in Paris at the moment? The anorak would go via Tunis without Fernand ever knowing and yet I also make him think about it. Yes, I make him, just as I make them all. Even if I sign myself "Mahu," there are four people involved, and if the concierge were to lock me up, she'd lock up everybody else as well, or what if her son steals the anorak and leaves before Coutin returns, all four of us would be robbed.

That's what being conscientious means. It's several people together and none of them being able to move without disturbing the others.

I then went down to the embankment to buy Ninette a Daumier engraving, not a real one, a reproduction, this rather amusing engraving is reproduced in a page of the magazine *Charivari*, it shows two women of the time bathing, they're wearing sort of clown's underpants and night-caps, one is fat and the other thin. There are others I remember looking at, such as *The Nymphs of the Seine*, showing great fat women floating on the river, and *Parisian Tritons, Male and Female*, which shows a man and his wife bathing, they have such faces! If you look behind the picture you can see it's a page out of a magazine, there are adverts, for example, for the Café des Amazones in the Passage de l'Opéra: "*You are waited on by Amazons. The only restaurant in Paris serving Suppers at 1 fr. 50.*" And the "*Suction teeth invented by Ges. Fattet. These teeth remain in place without the aid of either studs or clips and have none of the drawbacks of teeth costing 5 fr. which can never be used for mastication, as has been proved by numerous law-suits.*" And many adverts and all the other pictures I glanced at.

Now I come to think of it, did I steal them? Should I have bought them too? Supposing Daumier should remain in black and white, and not in the memory or in explanations? I'll ask Ninette if she thinks we should buy them all.

In spite of the pictures I'm still thinking about the anorak. What if Leaumont had asked Fernand and Fernand had signed himself "Mahu?" He would have made me think about it, I'd have been responsible, which all goes to show that anyone can be anything if someone thinks about you. I must go back to Coutin's and give him back the anorak with clean hands, I'll wait, I'll tear up the note that represents us all with my signature, I should have put "Leaumont" since it was he who gave me the anorak in the first place. Yes, I should have put "Leaumont," but I'll explain everything to Coutin, at least he won't be annoyed, I'll hold on to the note, I'll speak to him myself, it's safer than writing and leaving your friends to the mercy of a scrap of paper, out of negligence, and making them think about it out of negligence.

When someone thinks about me too much I have to ring him up or write to him telling him not to think about me, it's interfering with my work, I need to feel free.

I don't want anyone to think I'm a dishonest mischief-maker, I want people to say, "You're very conscientious."

24

Donnke Donnke Donnke

I used to have a temporary teacher for the cello when my own teacher was ill or rehearsing for a concert. I was given a very good education, music and all that. He was called M. Salvator. I think he was so broke my teacher took pity on him and gave him her own lessons when she was not free. He was fat, he had a beard and a moustache like Napoleon III's and a watch-chain. He would sit next to me, as I was trying to work at some Bach, and suck pastilles that smelled of wine-gums. He was always saying, "Donnke, donnke, donnke." That meant, "Enough of this squeaking and stumbling, let's begin again at the double crochets." He played very badly himself, as I realised when I asked him, "Would you play this passage for me?"

Donnke donnke donnke I'd begin again at the double crochets and it was getting on my nerves, I could smell the pastilles and I was sick of Bach, or Salvator.

My own teacher had a reddish pony-skin coat with a white pony-skin collar, I thought it was very smart. She used to come and give the lessons at my home. One day I pretended to be ill because I never practised enough and I got my sister to open the door. My teacher didn't sound very pleased and left. I caught a glimpse of her out of the window. But I think I was a bit ill, the afternoon dragged on, with the flowers on the wall picked out by the electric light and in the evening in my brown dressing-gown with yellow cuffs I felt I was going to be sick, it was the beginning of a bad cold, and I painted some bluish water-colours on poor-quality paper that soaked up the paint.

Don't you have silly memories like that? They're not very peculiar to childhood, I think, but rather to the beginnings of illnesses that are not very serious that are cured either by idleness or by the need for a holiday, you gain nothing from them, you get no pleasure out of them, I think, you just hang around with a taste of Famel syrup in your mouth.

She was nice, though, that music teacher, she thought I was very gifted, we gave her a box of chocolates at the New Year. Chocolate doesn't mean a thing to me now, my tastes have altered, nowadays I could eat potato salad for a month on end, it's cheaper and just as good as the *gratins* and soufflés we had at home. It's true, the taste of potatoes and oil with bread is so delectable, with no more than a pinch of salt. Supposing one day I eat too much potato, which sends me to sleep, then for three days I take nothing but coffee, which brings my stomach and nerves back to normal, long live coffee.

There are ideas that come to us through our fingers. You think of something as you warm your hands around your cup of coffee, all right, well, after a while you realise you're thinking of something else. You're dreaming about hot countries. And if at that moment you see an Arab in the street you think it's him who made you think about it, but it isn't, it's the cup.

Generally speaking, married people don't put themselves about. They don't have ideas any more, they're almost boring. I'm not saying one should always be cudgelling one's brains, what I mean is that always having a woman on hand makes you rather uninteresting.

25

New Photographs

There's an oratory, you know, near the bottom of the hill just before it gets steeper, I noticed as I was passing "*Forty days' indulgence for one Our Father and one Hail Mary*". That's really good value, more than a month, some people do a hundred or three hundred days, imagine, for three hundred days you're indulgent, you're good, people can kick you around and you turn the other cheek, yes it's certainly worth it, unless the prayer's too complicated. Pity one says "*indulgence*", I'd prefer "*dulgence*". Forty day's dulgence. It sounds more musical somehow.

We went to the fair to see the woman who weighs two hundred and eighty kilos, she was selling her photograph and saying, "Me Alsatian, me weigh nine kilos at birth." But the best thing was the dodgem-cars, I stayed there for ages, laughing to myself, I can't make other people laugh.

I like to pick up expressions here and there, for example, a woman says to a man, "Good morning, neighbour," or Poulet says to his sister-in-law who's expecting a baby, "Make sure it's a boy so that we can go and pee together," but there's an expression I don't like that I saw in a book-shop, "Seeking whom he may devour."

Do you like the sun? I like the hot sun in summer when you have no choice but to like it, but I hate the sun in winter, I even prefer my valleys to be grey and overcast in winter, that sort of weather suits me like a glove, I have a grey soul, not a sad grey, pearl grey. I'm also very fond of pear jam.

And while we're on the subject of geography and travelling, I think we'll have to invent a means of knowing all the languages in the world, why not through cigarettes? You smoke an English cigarette and you find you know English, or a Turkish cigarette and you know Turkish. Perhaps if you take those cigarettes that already exist and smoke them to the end, to the very end, so that there's no end left at all, it will work? I'll try it. Similarly, lots of pictures should be stuck to the wall that turn you into a fig-tree if it's a picture of a fig-tree or Toledo if it's of Toledo. And old records, you turn the handle and a voice starts singing, "*Gosse d'amour, t'es belle comme le jour,*" and you think it's you singing, perhaps because it's you turning the handle, anyway it's a rather depressing song.

I've stuck my new photographs in my album. They're just ordinary photographs. I cut off the white edges, I find it annoying having to focus between the white lines, I end up by seeing double, they reflect on to the scissors which jab into your thumb, the best way is to go straight for the picture itself, aiming as far away from the edge as possible as if you are making a jump on to a skiing track, too bad if you cut off a bit of the dark part as well. As I was sticking them in, I said to myself, "Heavens, here I am already living off my memories, aren't I going to get any further than this?" But no, it's just a stage in my life that is now put into perspective and stuck in an album to be looked at at some future time, and I can now set off again on the right foot. What difference does it make having a photograph album? Your life wouldn't be any more adventurous if you didn't have one. I'm sure Don Quixote had one, and those who die on battlefields are not indifferent to their memories. People who lead safe comfortable *petit-bourgeois* lives usually have no time even for a minimum of religious notions, under the pretext that it is bourgeois to be religious, but I have noticed that when you're in danger, on a rock-face for example, at an altitude of four thousand metres, you think quite instinctively of the odd bits of catechism you can remember. This being so, you should also, in strict honesty, think about them when you're not in danger. Though, goodness knows, buying your own house must be the greatest happiness in the world and I don't feel sorry for those who've known it.

26

Splitting Hairs

When I've lost all my hair, which I will if I take after my father, do you know what I'll do? I've a very simple solution: I'll grow a beard. It's so simple I'm amazed bald men haven't thought of it more often, it's compensation, you see hair on the face and you forget there isn't any one the head. It's an ugly sight a man without either hair or beard, it's disgusting. As I have a particularly full moustache and beard I'll have it cut in the Spanish style, I'll look like a figure in an El Greco painting, I know chaps who daren't grow a beard because of their wives or their families, I find that quite incomprehensible, as if there was something shameful or rude about a beard, they say that in their position it wouldn't be acceptable. If their position's so absurd, why do they stay in it? It's not a matter of making reforms, but of reforming oneself and being as one likes, isn't it.

I've seen young Pinson again, he's still as polite as ever, he's just come back from England, he met a girl over there, he says: "I ditched her straightaway, the first time we went out together I wondered what was wrong and I realised it was her voice, she had a nasal voice and never stopped asking questions. It was quite intolerable. It would have been better if she'd had a cold, a little catarrh might have softened her voice a bit. He said a lot of things like that that I found very amusing, such as: "What on earth do the English find to do on Sunday as they're sitting round their hearths? They probably organise family orgies under the photograph of the Queen. The slow pace of life there is pleasant up to a point," which reminds me of when I went to the London Fish Market. I got in the way of a porter carrying a load of oysters. In Paris I'd have been sworn at left, right and centre, but he just said "Oh, oh" very quietly so that I'd move out of his way.

Another chap I know is so polite he doesn't photograph people, even when they're asleep. I was out with him one day looking for typical views of the Pont-Neuf and I saw a *clochard* asleep near a big dog and a fisherman and I said to him, "Be quick, they'll move," but he wouldn't, he was afraid the *clochard* would wake up and the fishermen wouldn't be very pleased, but in fact it was because he daren't get any closer, as if people began at a distance of five metres and it would be indelicate to get any nearer.

27

Luxembourg Gardens

That's the last time I'm going to the dentist's, but I'm worried most of all about the bill. It's a new dentist I was told to go to, the old one's on holiday, he's a real brute, he didn't even put a towel under my chin, you just dribble on to your pullover. He gave me an injection, if it goes on like that I'll have nothing but dead teeth left, I'm terrified of having that death in my mouth even before he's done anything. Afterwards, I went on to the chemist's for Mlle Germaine, she's got pharyngitis, she doesn't belong to the social insurance either, she has to pay out five hundred francs for linctus and pills. I go and do her shopping for her in the freezing cold and she says it's too dear. "With that money, I could buy such and such a thing," she says. Funny reasoning.

If you're bored with my stories I don't care, I talk about what I know. On my way to the dentist I saw some men perched on the railings of the Luxembourg, they're re-doing the gold tips at the top, resoldering them, that's another pleasant little job, you're in the open air, you can watch people go by, you've hardly anything to do, and the spear-points are gilded.

A gym master was in charge of a gang of about thirty kids who were having a great time. "Raise your knees, higher, higher." They arrived at the little rose-garden in front of the orangery where it's a bit warm in winter, and the statue of Phidias which is so pretentious, has anyone thought of sticking Phidias on oranges, there's also Delacroix's fountain, it's so ugly, and I arrived at my dentist's in the Boulevard Saint-Michel. I had time to have a good look at the sitting-room, I quite like waiting, a carpet nailed to the floor, a large room, the wallpaper is deep pink and the woodwork brown with false beams on the ceiling gilt-edged like the doors, a green plant near the window and a gas-fire, which seems both old and clean, with a slight smell of sauerkraut that day, it was quarter-past two. Again he didn't give me a towel but I didn't dribble, I've still got a taste of cloves in my mouth.

I've tried to sell my cello again, the violin-maker in the Rue de Vaugirard gave me hopes, I took it to her thinking of the musical evenings we used to have in the musty little sitting-room at home, such a long time ago, but what does money care about that, poor old cello, I felt quite sorry for it, or is it because I can still almost hear that "Sicilienne" by Paradiès that I squeaked out, chromatic at first, my sister also playing wrong notes in the piano accompaniment, when I think of that "Sicilienne" I think first of those far-off wrong notes and secondly of the day I stumbled my way through it at a wedding.

28

Sweets

So I went to buy these snails. You can get them at those shops that sell all kinds of food and cold meats, or in a fish-shop next to the oysters, but I like the names of fish best of all, lemon sole, brill, red gurnard, weever, coalfish, sole, mullet, with big fresh bay-leaves around them and even carp caught yesterday and still breathing, they have a hard life. I'd like some rubber boots like the fishmonger's, you can't drag yourself away from a fish stall, it's a most exciting adventure, there are so many white fish in the sea. In the covered market I bought some grey snails and a bag of sweets for the concierge's little boy. I had a good laugh there because, imagine, it was evening, there weren't many people about, my right hand was holding the snails, and I held out my left hand and asked the woman to take thirty francs from my change and lo and behold if she doesn't whisper "How are you keeping, then?" I thought she was speaking to someone else. I looked round, there was no one. "Me?" I asked, bursting out laughing, but she said, "Sorry, I thought you were somebody else," anyone would have thought she was drunk, anyway, I was thinking afterwards, it was a way of getting into conversation. She looked at me out of the corner of her eye a bit, as if she wasn't quite sure, perhaps she thought quite simply that the familiar way in which I put out my hand had something more than familiar about it, perhaps she was used to certain gentlemen customers doing that, what if she was wearing glasses? It made me laugh so much! I regret having to laugh to myself sometimes, I'm very witty when I'm by myself.

This morning as I was having my coffee at the Cygne, I heard a customer getting angry, "My God! You've been serving me for six years and you still don't know!" He was having a rum and coffee, and it's true, the waiter must be some kind of imbecile, you have to tell him every day, "A strong white coffee," there's nothing more irritating. I understood how the customer felt better than anyone else who was there.

The lady psychiatrist or psychologist was at Latirail's yesterday to eat the snails, she said that when you tickle the soles of babies' feet they raise their toes instead of lowering them and the simple-minded are the same, it's a sign of non-evolution. I'd like to try to know how mature I am but it's not very amusing tickling the sole of one's own foot. I cooked the snails myself in a pan in which was some goose-fat left, the pan burst into flames. I was afraid the snails would be burnt but they were very good. The lady psychologist's husband cracked the shells open so that he could eat them all, some of them wouldn't come out of their shells, he's a very pleasant man this husband, with a broad face that looks as if it couldn't possibly look sad. His wife is also very pleasant. They were going to see *Les Enfants du Paradis* at the cinema, so we had to hurry with the meal.

Yet when I got home I ate all the concierge's sweets, it just happened to be what I had in the house. I like to have something to eat in the evening.

29

Deaf Children

I heard a good story in the cinema queue told by a chap who worked in an institution for deaf children, he was telling his friend that at Christmas all the children assembled in the hall and Father Christmas spoke to them in gestures and the children were very happy. You've got to imagine the silent scene. But meanwhile behind the curtain people were moving furniture and making a terrible row, of course it didn't matter as the children couldn't hear, but the chap who was telling the story could hear them and he watched this Father Christmas silently making his speech to the children. He told the story very well and I spent a most entertaining quarter of an hour waiting for my ticket. I find that a lot of people can tell stories, everybody in fact, but writing's different, it spoils everything, you've no voice, no eyes, it'll all be in vain, but when you speak you are even more real than what you have seen, because you explain things, you are both the ear and the brain of the person listening, but above all you are his eyes, you see through them, it's no effort to him, the story is alive because I'm alive beside him. Do you understand? I don't write for pleasure, but simply to invent people around me who will listen to me, otherwise why would I bother? I might as well be dead. You remember the story of the deaf children? You remember? Father Christmas making his gestures and the children listening to them, a long speech made as if they were all under water and on the other side of the curtain they're moving a piano or a side-board or God knows what with enough noise to burst their ear-drums, the chaps doing their work conscientiously . . .

The concierge's little boy comes and brings me my mail about quarter-past five, he's five, he rings the bell, I go to open the door and I find him quite pale and tense. He was afraid I wasn't there, he's just been painting. But every day I'm disturbed in this way, so now every other day or even several days in succession I go out at five o'clock so as not to be there. It's no use saying to him, "I haven't time," he goes in all the same. He puts his paper on the ground and does a quick sketch, like sausages over the whole sheet and if I ask him what it is, he says, "I don't know," but if I say, "It looks like Punch or a duck," he says, "Yes, that's right." I mix some paint for him and he puts some red or some green on one of the sausages, just a little, he wants to change the colour all the time, there's no end to it, I say to him, "That blue is very dear, put some on the other sausages, you mustn't waste it now it's been mixed." He then does another drawing and he asks, "Is this magnificent red very dear?" He says "Magnificent" just like me. One day I was sick of mixing red and I used some old fairly dry red in the box and I told him that this old red was the most beautiful of all, and now he wants only very old red.

30

The Poet and the Pineapple

On Sunday evening I sometimes go and have a *pot-au-feu* in a bistro round the corner that specialises in Sunday evening *pot-au-feu*, they don't serve meals in the week. About three metres away, leaning on the bar, was a sad-looking couple, a thin young man and a Spanish-looking girl, who looked very well dressed, but who probably had only one dress and one pair of shoes to her name; she had full lips and wore lipstick and had long red hair, I'm very fond of long hair. They seemed to be waiting for someone, they said a few words to each other every now and then, but I didn't catch what they said, perhaps they didn't want anyone to know why they were waiting, the waiter looked as if he didn't care. Another man, chubby-faced and wearing long socks, joined them then a girl in a navy-blue coat that was too long for her and short red socks, they both contrasted with the first two, they went on waiting. The badly-dressed girl went out and came back with a loaf, she held it out to her chubby-cheeked friend who ate a bit, but the tall thin one said he wasn't hungry, the well-dressed girl then went out and her friend opened the door for her and went back to the badly-dressed couple.

I went on eating my boiled beef and not knowing whether one ought to feel ashamed, when the well-dressed girl returned she whispered something to her friend and went and sat down at a table in the far corner, the two others followed and stayed standing near the table, watching them eat I think, I couldn't see properly at that angle. Suddenly the good-looking thin young man got up and, walking in a theatrical way to the bar, said, "I am a poet, Madame," and handed a piece of paper to the wife of the café owner, she read it and burst out laughing, it was probably some ribald madrigal, anyway she laughed and the poet smiled in a pained sort of way. He turned round and I saw a hole at the bottom of his trousers, he'd forgotten as he was waiting at the bar a little while before, but he'd remembered now that he was a poet, he'd said so, perhaps his madrigal would pay for his dinner. So you see, poetry can be useful, but it's important to forget your backside.

The people in these bistros on Sunday evening look very miserable unless they make an effort not to, they're on the look-out for the slightest thing to make them laugh, someone with double sight would be horrified to see what icebergs we are hidden in our clothes, trying to warm ourselves up with grinning beneath the neon lights.

In another dive I used to go to the landlady's face was covered in spots, her skin was like dried-up frog, and on top of the powder and dark orange lipstick, her hair was always curled on Sunday evenings and she had her best dress on, and the old servant who wore her grey hair long like a girl's was called Mme Marie, you ordered potatoes, and she'd go and call into the kitchen, "Chef, potatoes for one!", just like in an expensive restaurant.

You can't stop yourself completing people and objects in your imagination, without wishing to they make a sign that directs us to the secret like an arrow, but they can be deceptive sometimes, they don't want you to know. Seeing a friend of mine the other day wandering around the district with his wooden leg made me wonder what good it was to me having two real ones, I said to myself, "I'm in exactly the same boat, being alone is like having one leg less, which is why I get on well with cripples and half-wits."

The concierge's little boy drawing an apple-tree in a corner of his sheet of paper says, "The apple-tree makes apples" and sticking out his tongue he draws square apples with great concentration. Beneath the apple-tree is a donkey that looks more like a duck and a man without any shoes on. The kid can't be bothered to draw shoes as well and explains to me, "This man, his mummy doesn't want him to put shoes on because he wears out the toe-caps too quickly."

"Orange, apple, grapes, tomato, grapefruit, pineapple?"

recites the barman to some customers who want a fruit-juice. The customers choose grapefruit and pineapple. I wonder if it's like children who always repeat first what they hear last or whether it's because they prefer the exotic. Incidentally, I remember two Vietnamese in a greengrocer's, it was spring, there were spendid juicy cherries and strawberries, but the exiles chose a very expensive shrivelled pineapple, it was their country, their spring.

31

The Name

How do you think people manage who live under a false name? When they're hiding from the police I can understand, they pretend to be someone else while they're being looked for and they're very pleased when everyone's forgotten about them and they can get back to their real names, anyway they almost always tell their names to friends or to women they meet, it's only natural, when you take pleasure in something, you take it with your own skin, and not somebody else's, perhaps just once in passing, but next time it doesn't feel right, like in a carnival your disguise is amusing at the time but you're very pleased next day to get back to your old shirt and trousers, with your own smell, your name is your smell in a way, it sticks to you. I'm thinking of artists or actors, one day you read in the paper that the registrar of some town or other has registered the marriage of such and such a person, a pretty ordinary-sounding person, but this person is in fact the juggler well known under another name. So they have their own skin in the register office and in bed and another elsewhere? And which one would they have a boil on? I said juggler, it's the right word to describe him, or illusionist, it's the same with poets who put up a screen just to say I love you.

You have to stick to your name, you have to get used to the syllables, you should learn to master it so that it responds to the slightest gesture, you should live in it as in a house or a tent that you put up each night, it's too easy for those who put up another to sleep in, they wake up and find themselves in brocade instead of canvas, they've made a success of their song number or their trick with the pigeons, that is to say their life, and I don't admire them for it. But the rewards of sticking inside one's shell are great, for the ear that listens to the sound of the sea is your breathing.

I like words, a phrase heard in the street, any phrase, and I suddenly say to myself, "it's French, it's beautiful," I wasn't expecting it, because I'd have been less surprised if it had been in Tibetan, and the way you say good morning when it comes out fresh from your mouth like a sorbet, the voice is important too but that's another matter.

32

The Betting Office

On my way home I passed the P.M.U. betting office in the Rue Cambacérès, it was about three o'clock. I don't know anything about betting, I went in, there was a large blackboard on which women slip pieces of paper into pigeonholes, men with Astrakhan collars, white shirts and suède shoes, just like English lords, but there's nothing aristocratic about their faces, they're probably intermediaries; young men, old women sitting in their corners very knowledgeable about betting, holding their newspaper or their betting tickets, checking on bits of paper all kinds of arithmetical problems. I tried to read the regulations written up in the entrance, I went out and had a coffee in a café a few streets away and the waiter started talking quietly to a customer, I managed to catch the words, "Puységur . . . married a Cohen"; they too were in the game, the whole district at that time of the day breathes the air of the race-course. I went back to the betting office, they were still at it, passing tips to each other and when you look at them they speak out of the corner of their mouths to cover it up, but they were made, instead of number 19 as was thought it was 17 that won.

At the Place de la Concorde, just at the fork of the Cours la Reine, the traffic lights were at red and I saw a chap with a bunch of keys trying to open the switch-box, he was a criminal, no doubt about it, he glanced over his shoulder from time to time at the policeman who was busy directing the traffic, I stopped to watch him and I asked someone else who was watching, "What do you think he expects to find in there?" And he replied, "He probably wants to stop the traffic along a section of the avenue where his accomplices are posted to attack a car." I was most interested. I think it takes a lot of cheek to do a thing like that in the middle of the Concorde, I continued to watch the chap, he began to get annoyed, he couldn't open it, in the end he gave the box a couple of kicks and walked off. "The policeman ought to be warned," said my neighbour, but I thought that it was in bad taste to say that, on the contrary, initiative should be encouraged.

In the evening a friend came round to see me with a friend of his. "I'm going to a lecture, I've only got a minute," he said. He played a few chords on my guitar, the theatrical troupe he's just joined might be going to South America, he's taking lessons with a guitarist in a bar. He took a small parcel out of his case. "I've got some steaks," he said. "I've had them since yesterday evening, are they still fresh, in any case I can't eat them both this evening, would you like one?" I accepted in order to help him out but when he'd gone I thought to myself, "Fathead, he was only trying to be nice, he didn't know how to make you a present of a steak, he was embarrassed and made up the first excuse that came into his head."

33

A Child is Drawing

A child is drawing. He's being told a story. It goes from one ear to the other, it changes ear. If it's mine it stops there. It'll not see another ear again. I hear something buzzing around but I don't say anything. I keep it to myself. The story may go right round the world but no one will know. It's as well to tell a story in a very low voice, take precautions and it won't get any farther.

A child is drawing. He puts windows in a landscape. The windows have no houses. The child stays a long time at the window, he draws the curtain, he looks out, he draws trees, those branches, those branches, you scribble in green over the trunk, you scribble in a big ring that makes the leaves, you put in a lot of trees. All over the paper.

But where's that window gone, in the window that looks out he puts an eye. The trees are in the eye, they are green, they are in the fingers, they are on the paper. And the eye that wanders over all the trees is no longer in the window, it moves, it alights, it clings to the trunks, it clambers up to the leaves, it's no longer in school, it's everywhere. Lots of eyes. They see the window from afar off and say, "It's a window with us in it, it takes up the whole paper."

The child has stopped drawing. The mistress passes and stops. She sees the drawing, she leans over. She sees the windows without houses. She is surprised. She looks at the child. He's gone red in the face. He's got a silly face. Stupid child. Other schools didn't know what to do with him, so they let him draw, he changes the water in the fish tank, he takes out the fish with his bare hands.

The mistress looks closer and closer, there's the hasp, there's the curtain, she then looks out of the window, she doesn't see any trees. She sits down beside the red-faced child and looks at him. She can just make out something stirring in the child's eye. She asks him, "Have you finished drawing?" The child says yes. The mistress takes his paper away.

When it's time the children go out.

The mistress feels very cold. She puts on her thick winter coat, she's still cold, she puts the drawing into her bag, she goes home, she feels very ill, she goes to bed. She reaches out for her bag. She opens it. She takes out the drawing. She sticks it on the wall with a drawing-pin. She sees it at an angle because she can't raise her head from the pillow.

The child also went home. The doctor was there. His mother said to him, "Take your shirt off, doctor is going to give you a prick." He takes it off, the doctor gives the injection, the child doesn't say "ooh" and he puts on his shirt again.

But what stirred in the child's eye leaves the eye and goes back to the window. It stirs like a dandelion clock. You blow and phew! it's all blown away. It's almost too light. It settles anywhere at all. You see a lot of them get caught. They never reach the ground. You might say they were quite useless. They're doomed in advance. They just get swept away.

When the child went back to school he said to the mistress, "Miss, I had a prick for my glands yesterday."

The mistress put her hand on the child's head, she looked out of the window, she saw lots of trees with eyes wandering over them and she gave the drawing back to the child marked "Very good."

I keep what I'm told to myself. So much the worse for those who tell me things. So much the worse for their secret. From one ear to another. It's pointless.

34

The Negro

A negro is out walking one Sunday. He's got thick lips that won't close. He can't close them, they're too heavy.

He's in love with a white woman with thin lips that close properly. He is thinking about her. When he asks her, "Do you love me?" She hardly opens her mouth. Her lower jaw fits perfectly into her upper jaw. Her teeth fit so tightly together that when she shuts her mouth her cheeks move.

She's a white woman. She's very precise. She only says one thing at a time. Like a knife. She doesn't look very pleased when he asks her quite simple questions, such as, "Can you get your thumb into your navel?"

When you've got a mouth that doesn't shut properly it doesn't bother you at first. You've got so much to say that your mouth's always open. It's not noticeable. But if you fall in love it's terrible. You can't say anything any more. Your mouth's full, but it won't come out. And you can't shut it either. So it becomes noticeable. It bothers you. You do difficult exercises. You take advantage of being alone. You punch yourself in the face in the street all because of that region between Niamey and Sokoto that takes up too much room, that makes your jaw hang down. You notice it in shop-windows when you're walking in the street. You pretend you've got tooth-ache, you put your hand to your mouth. But you can't keep your hand to your mouth all day.

It's most upsetting. Your tongue's full of gazelles, your glottis is like a Baoule tam-tam and your saliva tastes like the Niger.

It's easy enough to shut your mouth with Paris inside, just Paris and the Boul' Mich'. But Africa's too big.

I met this negro near the Luxembourg Gardens. I was standing in front of a book-shop. I was looking at the flowers on a book-jacket. Whoever thought of putting flowers on a book-jacket? Printed flowers, of course. All the same, how ridiculous. Especially for the *Fleurs du Mal.* I said aloud, "Silly asses! As if flowers would make the book sell any better!" A negro who was standing beside me heard. He said, "That's true, it's grotesque, I see what you mean." We exchanged a few words. In the end I asked him what he was called.

"I daren't say."

"Why?"

"I'm called Mahu."

"Mahu? . . . But it's quite impossible. I know Mahu. He takes on various shapes, but I know him. He's a bit me under all his shapes. A bit me. I've never been a negro. I'm certain of that. I couldn't possibly be a negro. Especially with those magnificent lips you've got . . ."

"But I can't close them."

"All the more reason. I, a negro who can't close his lips? No, Monsieur, no. Tell me the truth."

"I tell you, I'm Mahu. He who clothes you in all his skins. Ah, you've got a long way to go yet! You're only at the beginning, at the very beginning. Mahu will have a long life. He'll go round the world, yes Monsieur, and under several shapes at once. I can already feel him becoming a pelican because of my mouth, a monkey because of my skull, a dromedary because of my hump . . . But we're looking too far ahead. Get used to this negro that we are. Let's not be embarrassed by our intimacy. But there's one thing we do not share. And that is a white woman I love. She's not yours. She's not even mine yet. But when I learn to shut this mouth of mine, perhaps . . ."

35

The Musée de l'Homme

It's a clever trick to say just what you see without adding anything, I like making things up but when I do people never understand what I say and stop listening. So, as I was walking in the street I passed some chaps who were removing some of that knock-down furniture, I was quite interested, but they looked at me as if to say, "What does he want? Why doesn't he move on?" and I can understand. When I see my face in a shop-window I look more like a pitchfork, it's very annoying, it's my eyes, they're pointed and always look worried, people don't like me to look at them, I wish I had eyes as soft as moths, they wouldn't bother anyone. Soft eyes are satisfied with each other, they don't need anything else to make them happy, but when I'm by myself I spend all my money at the cinema.

When you say something it's always a memory, in my opinion, even if it's made up, you see an incident that has just happened in your head, you spend your whole life looking back, even explorers I think, and especially poets since their job is to recount things. When I think of a picture of a poet I imagine him among other people turning round to remember the landscape. It's true, when I want to describe a person or an object at the time, I can't, it ties my tongue and petrifies my eyes, it's only afterwards you can describe or paint the blue of the sky, but then you have to go very slowly to make sure you've got it right, exactly as you want it.

I took the métro to Trocadéro to visit the Palais de Chaillot, it's so far. You never go there, when I got there I wanted to see the Musée de l'Homme, it would be a good opportunity, so I go in and, bang!, there I am in the middle of Mexico and the Totomacs, it's quite a shock. Pre-Columbian civilisations, with such magnificent names, I'd like to have written them down but I hadn't got a pencil, you look, you go through the different rooms, you forget your geography, you go round the world and I find myself trembling in front of mummies from Ecuador. That's one thing I don't like about museums: What should you look at most? There's a coffin as big as a Norman cupboard, red, in carved wood decorated with swans' feathers, and masks, people pulling faces everywhere. Coming out I begin to think that Man must be pretty crazy, I say to myself, "So that's the human spirit, it's wonderful when you think about it, the world is pretty big, you have to admit," and I felt how silly I was with my own little ideas.

36

What importance . . . ?

When you shave you see that life is dark. You put soap on your cheeks, you lather your cheeks, you lather, under your nose, under your chin, on your cheeks, you lather your cheeks, on your nose, you lather your forehead you lather, you lather and all you've got left are your eyes and a narrow strip around your eyes, and this narrow strip is dark, it's your skin, all that's left is this very dark skin around the eyes, am I a redskin, no it's my living skin. It's so dark!

It's a strange thing, you shave every day and it's only today you notice a thing like that.

It's strange, what importance would you give to that little strip around the eyes, you there, in front of me, shaving? Why not your eyes as well, why don't you lather over your eyes? But I'm afraid of that skin that looks at me, it stands out by itself in the mirror, what if I cut it with my razor? A razor to cut the eyes out with, I shave, shave and Crrc nothing in front of me.

I'm afraid of it slipping, careful, good God, why, it's the same for everyone, we've all got these little rings that we don't shave, every day everyone confronts his own eyes?

Pull a face. Unless you're afraid to, all right. Otherwise cut your eye, then cut your other eye and tomorrow when you want to shave you'll ask someone to help you. Nothing more to remember. People will tell you what they see. And you'll think, "If only I had known what little importance to give to my skin, to my eyes . . ."

I wonder if it would be better to keep this dark life, this little strip of skin all your life or just cut, shave, and get someone to guide you around. People would say to you, "There's someone here you can't see, you're blind, but I assure you, someone who looks just like you."

37

The Key

No need to lie any more, I lied a great deal at the beginning of this book in order to get to this point, to arrive at the truth, which proves that truth emerges from an inextricable confusion, I wanted it to be like that, I don't deny anything, not even a difference of speech. And all my characters that are now so far away, they were just the material, and their adventures were really my adventures and Mahu is really me and I don't carry parcels any more but sit down with a pen and an exercise-book. Some of the characters, such as Latirail and Ninette, really are friends of mine, they weren't at first, but they were in the end, except that I gave them false names, for which I apologise, truth ripens only in the last chapter.

Between you and me, the first part was a novel that didn't work out but it doesn't matter, it gave me a few scales to practise on, what matters to me is not that I should sing well, but that I should hear my voice without bronchitis, when you've got bronchitis, you know, there are lots of little whistling noises.

Well, there you are, I've nothing else to say, but the game's mine, I've won.